AIN'T NO BREAKIN' US!

The Block Raised Them. Love Changed Them.

TEAMA HERICE

DEDICATION

To my incredible husband, Wickly –

You are still my rock, my safe place, and my greatest cheerleader. Through every late-night writing session, every plot twist, and every moment of doubt, you've been my steady hand and my calm in the storm. Your quiet strength speaks louder than any words, and your love keeps our family standing tall. I am blessed beyond measure to walk this life with you.

To my amazing oldest son, Justin –

You continue to lead with wisdom, courage, and heart. You're more than a big brother—you're a protector and an example of what it means to stand firm in love. Watching you grow into the man you are today fills me with pride so deep it's hard to put into words. Keep shining, son—the world needs your light.

To my sweet baby boy, Tyson –

Your bravery still inspires me every single day. Tyson's Big Brave Heart was only the beginning—this new chapter in life and love is just as much yours as it is mine. You've taught me that strength isn't about size, but about the heart behind it. Thank you for reminding me that even the smallest voices can make the loudest impact.

To my incredible nieces, Maniece and Li'Byra

You are growing into young women who light up every room you walk into. Your laughter still fills my spirit, and your creativity reminds me that dreams have no limits. Always remember—you are powerful, you are worthy, and you are deeply, deeply loved.

To my family—my circle of love, my unshakable foundation—

You are my reason and my reminder that nothing in this world is stronger than the bond we share. May these words forever echo the truth: Ain't no breaking us.

With all my love,

TeAma Herice

<h1 style="text-align:center">ABOUT THE AUTHOR</h1>

TeAma Herice is a writer   rooted in the raw truths of   love, struggle, and survival. Raised around the rhythms and realities of   the neighborhood, TeAma writes stories that shine light on loyalty, friendship, and the messy but powerful journey of finding love where the odds are stacked against it. With a voice that   blends grit, honesty, and heart, TeAma brings readers into worlds that feel lived-in, authentic, and unforgettable.

When not writing, TeAma draws inspiration from family,   community, and the pulse of everyday life—always chasing stories that prove love can grow strong even in the toughest soil. Ain't No Breakin'   Us is a testament to that spirit: raw, real, and unshakable.

Website: www.cantputdown.com

Email: cantputdown01@gmail.com

<h1 style="text-align:center">ACKNOWLEDGMENTS ⟫◇◇◇◇◇◇⟨</h1>

Whew—what a journey this has been! Tyson's Big Brave Heart didn't just come from a place of imagination, it came from a place of deep love, faith, and the powerful encouragement of the people around me.

To my bestie, my forever friend, Herman "Junior" Callwood –

What would life be without your laugh, your wisdom, and your ability to keep it real even when I don't want to hear it? You've been by my side through every high, every low, and every "you got this" moment. Thank you for being the shoulder I lean on, the one who reminds me of who I am when I forget, and for loving me like family. I cherish our bond more than words can express. You've held me down, lifted me up, and stayed true— mushed up for life!

To my brother in spirit and literary fire, Anthony P. Brown –

Whew! Where do I even begin? Your success lit a fire in me. Watching you write, publish, and share your truth gave me the courage to believe in mine. You never let me settle, never let me sit in self-doubt. You reminded me that my voice matters, my stories matter, and that I was born to do this. Your push, your presence, and your example changed my life. Thank you for pouring into me the kind of motivation that breaks chains and births books. You didn't just open the door—you held it wide open and said, "Sis, it's your turn now." I'll never forget that.

To my ride-or-die sister in heart, Anya Dayton-Burrs –

From our first laugh to our deepest talks, you have been my safe place. You've celebrated my wins like they were your own, cried with me when life hit hard, and reminded me that friendship is a gift that grows stronger through every season. Your unwavering love, fierce loyalty, and constant encouragement have been my anchor. I thank God for blessing me with a best friend like you.

To my soul sister, Charmaine Brown –

Girl, where do I start? You are that rare kind of friend who sees the real me, even in my quietest moments, and loves me harder because of it. You've spoken life into me, prayed over me, and reminded me of my worth when I was too tired to fight for it myself. You are proof that family isn't always by blood—it's by heart. I am so grateful   for your light, your strength, and your unwavering belief in me.

To everyone who believed in me,   supported me, read the early drafts,   or simply asked, "How's the book coming?" — thank you. Your words kept me writing on the days when I wanted to quit.

To every child, every parent, every family member who has ever struggled to find the right words to say "I'm proud of you" or "you're doing just fine"—I wrote this for you too.

This book was created with love,   with courage, and with the unshakable support of a village that refused to let me give up. I pray it touches hearts, opens minds,   and reminds every reader,   young and old,   that bravery doesn't mean having no fear—bravery means showing up anyway.

With all my love and gratitude,

TeAma Herice

TABLE OF CONTENT

CHAPTER BREAKDOWN

1. **"Same Block, Same Story"**
    Introduce Nia and Jay's friendship, daily grind, neighborhood life.

2. **"The Test That Changed Everything"**
    Nia finds out she's pregnant. Ex walks away. Jay offers quiet support.

3. "Rides & Late Nights"
    Jay gives Nia rides, they talk, old sparks show — neither admits it.

4. **"Whispers & Side-Eyes"**
    Neighborhood gossip starts. Jay's ex, Erica, watches from the sidelines.

5. **"Lines Getting Blurry"**
    An unexpected intimate moment — tension rises, but both pull back.

6. **"Old Wounds, New Fears"**
    Nia pushes him away, scared. Jay tries to stay cool but struggles.

7. "Truth Don't Hide"
    A raw argument — Jay confesses he's been in love with her.

8. "Taking That Step"
    They decide to try — awkward, messy, but hopeful.

9. "Pressure from All Sides"
    Money tight, family drama, Erica's games — tension boils.

10. **"Scared But Standing"**
    Pregnancy complications — they face it together, fears and all.

11. **"Our Little World"**
    Baby arrives. Small, beautiful moment — not perfect, but real.

12. **"Always Been You"**
    Final scene — them as a family, still fighting, still loving, still standing.

CHAPTER 01

Same Block, Same Story

The fan above Jay's bed squeaked with every slow rotation, its blades stirring up the thick, humid air — making more noise than cooling. Morning sunlight bled through warped blinds, casting faded stripes across walls marked with posters of muscle cars, worn Polaroids, and scuffed drywall from years of fists meeting frustration.

The mattress dipped as Jay sat up, elbows on his knees, head hanging low. Sweat already clung to the back of his neck — West Palm didn't care it wasn't even 9 am. yet. The heat came early, stayed late, pressed in like a second skin.

His phone buzzed, rattling across the chipped surface of his nightstand, vibrating against a socket wrench and an unopened pack of Black & Milds that never left his side.

Marcus: Pick me up later. Court.

Jay sighed. No please, no thank you, just like always. He thumbed the message away, not bothering to reply yet. Same brother, same problems. Court dates, empty promises. He'd deal with that later.

Outside his cracked window, the neighborhood was already wide awake. The sharp pop-pop-pop of a basketball echoed through the complex. A lawnmower droned in the distance. From across the lot, someone was frying bacon — the sizzle floating on the breeze, tangled with the faint, salty breath of the ocean that never quite reached their side of town.

The apartments across the lot looked the same faded beige they'd been since Jay could remember — sun-bleached, graffiti-tagged in corners, wires dangling like spiderwebs overhead. Paint chipped from the railings, laundry flapped on makeshift lines strung between rusted poles. The whole place looked tired — like it had seen better days and didn't expect to see them again anytime soon.

But it was home.

Jay stood, muscles loose but heavy from yesterday's work — a long day under cars at the shop, grease still stubbornly clinging under his nails. His plain white tee was crumpled on the chair by the door; he pulled it on, ran a hand over his short waves, then grabbed his boots. Lacing them slow, methodical — the way his uncle taught him when he was a kid: "Double knot 'em. Life will try to trip you up enough — don't help it along."

Keys jingled in his palm as he stepped outside, the apartment door clicking shut behind him.

Heat smacked him in the face like it   owed him money.   The concrete beneath his boots was cracked, weeds sprouting through jagged lines like nature refusing to be ignored. Over by the basketball   court, a group of kids played a sloppy game — deflated ball, rim bent to hell. The youngest — big ears, small frame — spotted Jay.

"Aye, Jay! Lemme ride in the Mustang!" the kid called, voice cracking with hope.

Jay smirked, tugging his hat lower against the sun. "You still   can't make a layup, lil' man. Dream smaller."

The kid groaned as the ball clanked off the backboard, proving Jay's point.

Jay's Mustang sat near the corner, black paint dulled from the sun but still mean-looking, low to the ground,   chrome rims biting the sunlight.   Pride swelled in his chest   just seeing her. She wasn't showroom perfect — a couple dings, an old engine — but   she was his. Paid for with late nights, grease-stained hands,   and enough hustle to make something out   of nothing.

Keys in hand, Jay approached, already thinking about the day ahead — oil changes, busted transmissions, Marcus's damn court   mess — when he heard her.

The voice cut through the morning noise like it was wired into his bones. "Come on, man… don't play with me right now…"

Jay froze for half a second, lips pulling into a slow, crooked grin.

There she was.

Across the lot, by her beat-up Honda Civic,   stood Nia Williams — arms crossed, jaw tight, brows pinched in frustration. Her curls were piled on top of her head in a messy bun,   a few stubborn strands falling across her forehead. Gold hoops caught   the sun as she shifted,   muttering curses under her breath. Tank top hugging her curves, jeans ripped at the knees, Air Maxes scuffed but still clean.

Jay leaned against the hood of his car, watching her work the key in the ignition again. The Civic coughed, sputtered, then fell silent like it had given up on life.

Nia slapped the steering wheel. "Stupid-ass car…"

Jay's grin widened, amusement warming his face as he shook his head.

Some things never changed.

For years — since middle school,   since high school parties, since every low point and dumb argument and messy ex in between — it had been like this. Her, stubborn and loud. Him, steady and watching. The world spinning wild, but them? Always orbiting the same block,   the same corners,   the same complicated space between just friends and something else.

Jay exhaled, pushing off the Mustang.

"Here we go," he muttered,   making his way across the lot,   heat rising off the pavement, heart stumbling quiet and familiar in his chest as he headed straight for the one person in the neighborhood who could still throw him off balance.

The air in the lot was thick with heat and the faint sting of engine oil. Jay's boots hit the pavement slow as he crossed toward her,   every step quiet, steady — the way you approach something dangerous you still   can't stay away from.

Nia's back was turned,   curls bouncing as she muttered under her breath and twisted the keys in the ignition one last   time. The Civic wheezed, coughed, and died, the engine letting out   one final, pitiful sigh like it had given up on life altogether.

Jay grinned to himself, the corner of his mouth lifting slow. Same old Nia… same old Civic… same old headache.

"Car giving' you attitude again, huh?" he called out, voice cutting across the lot like the low hum of tires on hot concrete.

Nia flinched just   a little,   then groaned,   head falling back against   the headrest in pure exasperation.

"Lord, not you," she mumbled, eyes closing for a beat.   Then she cracked one open to glare at him. "You always pop up right when I'm ready to cuss something out."

Jay shrugged, crossing his arms as he leaned a shoulder against the door frame, peering in through the window.

"Maybe it's karma.   Or maybe it's the fact   your car's got more problems than the entire block combined."

"Funny," Nia deadpanned, slipping the keys out of the ignition and shoving them into her   purse. She pushed the door   open, sliding out, her legs brushing against his for just a second — skin warm from the sun, the faint scent of coconut oil and something sweet trailing with her.

Jay stepped back a fraction, more out of self-preservation than politeness. "Look at you," he teased, nodding toward the Civic. "She ain't even tryin' to start no more. Gave up like your last man."

Nia's eyes cut sharp toward him, a flash of amusement under the attitude. "You wanna get   cussed out   first thing in the morning?"   she shot back, folding her arms across her chest. Her gold bangles clicked softly with the movement. "'Cause I will hurt your little mechanic feelings."

Jay laughed low, the sound rumbling deep in his chest   as he popped the hood. "Go 'head. Been a minute since somebody tried."

She followed, arms still crossed, watching as he leaned under the hood, brow furrowing at the sad state of the engine.

"You know this thing's basically running'   on prayer, right?" he said after a second, poking at a loose wire with practiced fingers.

"Yeah, well, prayer's cheaper than a new car,"   Nia muttered, kicking a loose rock near her foot. The corner of her lip twitched — tired, frustrated, but still fighting to keep her walls up.

Jay straightened, wiping his palms on his shirt.   His eyes lingered on her face a little longer   than they should've — the soft   curve of her jaw, that stubborn set to her mouth.

"You riding' with me," he declared, shutting the hood with a dull clunk.

"I'm fine," Nia shot back on instinct, even though they both knew she wasn't.

"Ni," Jay said, voice dropping low, all the teasing stripped away now. "It's already ninety degrees. You walking' to work, or you letting' me drive you?"

Nia opened her mouth, pride loaded and ready to fire, but then her eyes drifted to the Civic — tired, beat-down, giving her no backup in this argument.

She sighed, reaching into her bag and fishing out her keys. "Fine. But I pick the music."

Jay unlocked the Mustang with a click, holding the passenger door open for her with a cocky little tilt of his head. "Yeah, yeah. But no Megan Thee Stallion. I'm not trying hear hot-girl anthems before I've had my coffee."

Nia grinned despite herself, sliding into the passenger seat. The leather was warm, the faint scent of air freshener and motor oil filling the car. Her shoulder brushed his as she settled in, the contact brief but heavy.

Jay walked around to the driver's side, taking his time, eyes lingering on her reflection in the side mirror — her eyes scanning the neighborhood, guarded as always, chin lifted like she dared the world to come at her today.

Sliding into the driver's seat, Jay started the engine, the deep rumble of the Mustang filling the air.

Same block. Same damn block.

But sitting next to her? It never got old. And maybe… just maybe… today, something was different.

The Mustang's engine rumbled low as Jay eased out of the lot, tires crunching over loose gravel, the sun already hanging heavy in the sky like it had something to prove. The air inside the car
was warm, thick with the faint scent of leather, old air freshener, and that trace of coconut oil drifting off Nia's skin.

She flipped through radio stations with casual authority, one hand dancing over the console, fingers tapping to a rhythm only she could hear.

"Lemme guess," Jay muttered, keeping one hand steady on the wheel, eyes fixed on the road. "You about to put on that headache you call music and ruin my speakers."

Nia side-eyed him, a slow grin creeping across her face. "Correction. I'm about to save your tired playlist from itself."

She landed on a station — bass thumping heavy, hi-hats slicing sharp through the mix. Some South Florida trap bled through the speakers, the kind with enough bass to shake your lungs loose.

Jay winced, exaggerated. "See, that's exactly why your car hates you. Bad energy."

"My car hates me 'cause she's old and tired," Nia shot back, adjusting the volume with a twist of her wrist. "Kinda like you."

Jay chuckled under his breath, turning onto the main street. "Nah, I age like wine."

"You age like expired milk," Nia quipped, lips curving into a satisfied grin as she leaned back in the seat.

Jay shook his head, fighting the real smile threatening to break through.

The car rolled through the neighborhood, windows cracked just enough to let the thick air drift in. Outside, the world passed in slow, familiar snapshots — Miss Delores sweeping her porch in slippers and a bonnet, old men posted outside Rico's bodega trading gossip and lottery numbers, a kid in a faded Spider-Man shirt running barefoot down the cracked sidewalk.

Palm trees leaned crooked against the sky, their leaves whispering in the sticky breeze. The buildings looked tired — paint peeling, screen doors hanging loose, rust crawling up fences — but it was home. Always had been.

They rode in easy silence for a moment, the music filling the gaps, bass vibrating soft underfoot. But the tension? That lived quiet in the spaces between words, in the way Jay's eyes kept flicking sideways — catching the set of Nia's jaw, the tight line of her mouth, the crease between her brows she always got when life pressed too hard.

"You good?" he asked finally, voice low, calm, but real.

Nia kept her gaze on the passing street, curls brushing her shoulder as she shrugged. "I'm good."

Jay didn't buy it.

"You sure? 'Cause your car's one bad day away from the scrapyard,   and you look like you ain't slept in two weeks."

Nia let out a short laugh, sharp around the edges. "Wow, you just full of compliments today."

"Just calling' it how I see it."

She stayed quiet,   eyes on the world sliding past   — the boarded-up laundromat, the faded mural of palm trees and sunsets somebody painted years ago, now chipped and worn.

Finally, she sighed. "It's life, Jay. You know how it is."

Jay's grip on the wheel tightened. He did know. Better than most.

"Work still kicking' your ass?" he asked, turning down a side street.

"Two jobs, one apartment, zero rich uncles," Nia muttered, adjusting the strap of her bag.

 "Ain't nobody out here saving me."

The bitterness in her voice was soft, but it cut deep — worn in, like it lived under her skin.

"You don't need saving," Jay said, eyes still on the road. "But you do need to stop trying carry the whole damn world by yourself."

Nia tilted her head, eyes narrowing slightly. "You sound like my grandma."

"I sound like somebody who's known you since braces and that   busted side ponytail," Jay countered, lips twitching at the memory.

Nia groaned, sinking lower in the seat.   "Why you got   to bring up old trauma?"

Jay laughed, a deep rumble loosening his chest. "Point is, Ni... you ain't got to do everything alone. You know I got you."

Her eyes met his briefly — quick, searching — then slid away. "Yeah," she murmured, voice soft.

"I know."

But Jay could feel the walls still standing between them, tall and stubborn, built brick by brick over the years. It wasn't just the neighborhood or the exes or the struggle. It was them — too proud, too scared to risk messing up what they already had.

They pulled up outside her job — a sneaker shop squeezed between a cell phone repair place and a rundown barbershop. Faded posters filled the windows, advertising sales nobody noticed.

Jay cut the engine. The car rumbled into silence.

Nia grabbed her bag, pausing with one hand on the door handle. For a second, neither of them moved — the air thick, music still humming faint from the speakers.

"Thanks for the ride," she said finally, voice softer now, stripped of attitude, walls down just enough for him to glimpse the tired beneath.

Jay nodded, eyes lingering on hers. "Anytime."

A heartbeat stretched between them — full of all the things they never said, all the feelings stuffed down because friends was safer than what if.

Then Nia opened the door, stepping out into the heat, curls bouncing as she adjusted her bag.

Jay watched her go — the sway in her hips, the steel in her spine, the sharp edges and softness tangled together in one person who'd been driving him crazy for years without even trying.

The bell above the shop door jingled as she disappeared inside, and just like that, the car felt too quiet.

Too empty. Too still.

Jay exhaled slow, fingers tapping the wheel as the engine idled back to life.

Same block. Same damn story.But every time she looked at him like that… every time her   voice softened like that… it   felt like maybe, just maybe, something was gonna change.

CHAPTER 02

The Test That Changed Everything

The bell over the sneaker shop door gave its same tired jangle as Nia stepped inside, the weight of her bag dragging at her shoulder. The faded glass still read Sole Stop, though the S had peeled away so it looked more like Ole Top. Pretty much summed up the place—old, tired, barely holding on.

Rows of Jordan's, Forces, and Vans lined the walls, most locked behind plexiglass. A weak fan buzzed near the register, fighting a losing battle against the Florida heat bleeding in through the door.

Nia slid behind the counter and dropped her bag to the floor with a soft thud. Her whole body felt off—limbs heavy, head foggy, stomach knotted with a dull ache that had been building for days. She blamed stress, long hours, maybe that greasy food from Rico's last night. But deep down, she knew better. She just wasn't ready to face it.

"Girl, you look like you walked here from Miami," Tasha's voice called from the back, thick with that messy cousin energy only she could bring. Her acrylic nails clicked against her phone screen as she leaned on a stack of Nike boxes, gum snapping loud between her teeth.

Nia groaned, grabbing her apron from the hook. "I feel like I walked here from Miami."

Tasha's eyes scanned her, sharp and unrelenting. "You eat this morning?"

"Nope."

"You sleep?"

"Barely."

"You late?" The teasing dipped low, but there was real concern underneath.

Nia tied the apron behind her waist, glaring. "I'm tired, not pregnant."

But the words tasted bitter, like her mouth already knew the lie.

Tasha didn't press—yet—but her look said she wasn't convinced. She snapped her gum again, grabbing a price scanner, her acrylics clacking against the plastic. Trap music hummed low through the speakers, too weak to drown out the tension building in Nia's chest.

The shop wasn't busy yet. A couple of customers browsed: an older man
inspecting socks like they were treasure,   a teenage boy hovering near the
Air Max display, probably rehearsing how to convince his mom to buy them.

Outside, the sun blazed against the glass, casting sharp rectangles of light
across the faded floor   tiles. The street pulsed with its usual rhythm—car
horns, screeching tires, someone yelling in Spanish down the block.

Nia rubbed her temple, begging her body to hold up through just one more
shift. But her stomach churned. Her chest tightened. Her skin felt clammy.
It had been like this for days— waves of exhaustion, nausea circling at the
edges, her body whispering truths she didn't want to hear.

The bell over the door chimed again.

A young dude swaggered in, sunglasses still on, phone glued to his ear.

His voice boomed across the small store.

"Yeah, nah, she tripping'. I told her I don't even know that chick—"

Nia sighed, already bracing herself.

The dude barely looked at her. "Yo, them new Dunks in?"

"Over there," she said,   sliding customer service into her voice, pointing
toward the display.

He wandered off, still arguing into his phone.

Tasha drifted over, low enough so only Nia could hear. "He looking'   for the
Dunks but can't find loyalty."

Nia snorted, lips curling despite herself. "Stop."

The next hour dragged. Customers filed in loud, impatient, more interested
in flexing than buying. A woman argued over the return policy.   A group of
teens hovered by the slides, cracking jokes, leaving fingerprints across the
plexiglass.

Through it all, Nia's head swam.

She counted change, folded socks, answered the same tired questions, but the feeling kept pressing in. Her hands trembled faintly at the register. The room tilted just enough to scare her.

Sweat beaded along her hairline despite the weak AC rattling above. Tasha spotted it instantly.

"You good?" she asked, her voice stripped of teasing now.

"I'm fine," Nia said, too quick. Her fingers clenched the counter as if it could steady her.

She wasn't fine.

And deep down, she already knew why. The door clicked shut behind Nia with a quiet finality, the soft hum of the old air-conditioning unit filling the apartment as she leaned back against it, eyes slipping closed for a second.

The weight of the day pressed down on her chest—long hours on her feet, customers with attitudes, her stomach twisted in knots that had nothing to do with food.

The familiar scent of lavender clung to the secondhand couch, the thin curtains, the worn throw blanket slung over the armrest. Her little apartment—barely big enough for her and her stubborn pride—felt smaller tonight.

Streetlights buzzed faintly through the blinds, casting broken stripes of orange across the floor. A car rolled by, bass thumping low through the walls, rattling the windowpanes before the neighborhood settled quiet again.

Nia slipped off her sneakers, one foot after the other, toes curling against the cool tile. Her legs ached, her lower back stiff from standing too long behind the register, plastering on fake smiles for people who couldn't care less.

She crossed to the couch, dropping her bag onto the cushion with a tired thud. The worn fabric sagged under the weight, the bag slumping open like it, too, had given up for the day.

For a long moment, she just stood there, staring down at it—the cracked leather strap, the faded edges—fingers flexing at her sides like they didn't know what to do.

Her stomach churned again.   Not sharp. Not overwhelming. Just that dull, persistent roll of unease that had been riding her for days.

She exhaled slow, sinking onto the couch,   the cushions dipping beneath her as she pulled the bag into her lap and tugged the zipper open.

Receipts, lip gloss, gum wrappers, loose change, her phone dead at the bottom. She fished through the clutter until her fingers brushed it.

The box.

Small. Plain. White and blue lettering.   The quiet weight of the unknown pressed into her palm.

Pregnancy test.

Her throat tightened.

Tasha's voice echoed in the back of her head, that no-nonsense tone only cousins who knew all your business could perfect: "Just take it. If you ain't pregnant, cool. But you gone' sit here stressing' yourself out for what? You know your body, Nia."

And she did. That was the part that scared her.

The fatigue. The nausea creeping in.   The way her jeans felt tighter last week. The missed period she tried to blame on stress.

Denial had worked for days. But now? The truth sat   heavy in her palm, staring her down.

Her heart thudded steady in her chest,   her pulse loud in her ears as she turned the box over,   reading the instructions like they might   somehow change.

Two lines. Positive.

One line. Negative.

Simple. Final. No room for maybes.

Her mouth went dry as she set the box on the coffee table, fingers lingering on the cardboard before she pulled back like it burned her.

The apartment hummed quiet around her. The AC clicked on and off.

Distant voices drifted through the cracked window—somebody laughing,   a car door slamming, a low conversation in Spanish from next door.

But inside her little living room, time slowed to a crawl.

Fear curled in her gut, tight and sharp.

She wasn't ready for this.

But ready or not, it was happening.

Nia pushed off the couch, legs stiff as she grabbed the box with trembling fingers and headed toward the bathroom.

The plastic test clicked against the edge of the sink as she set it down with careful, trembling fingers.

The bathroom was small—barely enough space to turn without   bumping the wall—but suddenly it felt enormous. The air stretched thick, heavy with humidity and the weight of what she was about to know.

The mirror caught her reflection again: wide brown eyes rimmed with panic, curls frizzed from the heat, a faint sheen of sweat on her forehead.

Her heart thudded, slow but hard, each beat vibrating through her chest like it wanted out.

The instructions were simple.   Black and blue lettering,   sterile and final: "Hold for five seconds.   Wait three minutes. Two lines: Positive. One line: Negative."

Three minutes.

But fear stretched them into an eternity.

She sank onto the closed toilet lid, elbows braced on her knees, chin in her hands. Her eyes stayed fixed on the small plastic window on the counter.

Still blank.Her mind spiraled.

It's just stress. It's just the heat. It's just… life.

But deep down? Her body had been whispering the truth for days—soft at first, then louder, creeping into her bones with every wave of nausea, every missed day on the calendar, every stretch of exhaustion that sleep couldn't touch.

The test would confirm it. One way or another.

Her eyes drifted to the mirror's corner, where a faint crack spider webbed through the glass—a leftover from the day she'd slammed the door too hard during an argument with Marcus.

Marcus.

His voice, his laugh, his charm that filled a room like smoke—then disappeared just as fast when things got too real.

The father.

Assuming he picked up his phone.

Nia's jaw clenched. Seconds crawled by, her pulse loud in her ears, the faint hum of the light buzzing overhead.

Her foot tapped an uneven rhythm on the cracked tile. Her palms dampened.

She rubbed them down her thighs, forcing herself to breathe.

Two lines. Positive.

One line. Negative.

The math was simple. The reality wasn't.

Finally, she stood, legs unsteady as she crossed to the sink.

Her fingers hovered, then grabbed the test, flipping it over.

Two pink lines.

Clear. Sharp. Undeniable.

Her throat went dry, her chest tightening like a fist curled around her rib-cage and squeezed.

Pregnant.

No more guessing.   No more pretending.   No more blaming stress or exhaustion or the heat.

The truth sat heavy in her hand, two lines shouting louder than words.

Her mind scrambled, racing through what came next—doctor appointments, telling her grandma, telling Marcus, the rent she barely made, the two jobs she juggled, the dream of beauty school she kept tucked in the back of her mind.

Now? That "maybe" felt a million miles away.

Nia's knees buckled as she lowered herself back onto the toilet lid, the test still in her hand, her eyes burning with tears.

She wasn't ready.

But ready or not, it was happening.

The apartment pressed in—the hum of the AC, the creak of the building, the street noises drifting through thin glass.

Life outside kept moving.

But in here? Everything stopped.

The test sat on the counter, those two pink lines etched into her memory now.

Nia drifted back into the living room.

The faint lavender air freshener, the hum of the old AC, the sag in the middle of her couch—it was all the same, but smaller. The walls pressed in like they were closing inch by inch.

Her phone buzzed beside her, cracked screen lighting up with the last conversation she never finished.

Marcus.

Unanswered messages.

"You good?"

"Let me know when you around."

"We need to talk."

Read. Ignored.

The last one was two days old, the little "Delivered" beneath it untouched.

Same old Marcus. Sweet when he wanted to be. Quick with promises that cracked under pressure. Gone when life tilted too far into the real.

Her thumb hovered over the call button.

She didn't want to need him. But this wasn't about pride anymore.

With a shaky exhale, she tapped. The call rang.First ring.

Second.

Third.

No answer.

"Yo, it's Marcus. You know what to do."

Beep.

The silence after the beep pressed in, daring her to leave the words.

But memory stopped her   cold. The excuses,   the ghosting that   always followed.

He wasn't here now. He hadn't been there then.

And some part of her already knew… he wasn't coming.

She pressed End, the screen going black.

Tears burned, but pride shoved them back down.

This was her fight now. Like always.

A knock echoed through the apartment, sharp and steady, cutting through the quiet.

Her heart jumped.

Another knock—three measured taps and a pause.

Jay.

Of course. Nobody else knocked like that.

Nia's stomach twisted, the test still sitting in the bathroom like a shadow she couldn't outrun.

She hesitated at the door, hand flat against the cool wood. Part of her wanted to stay quiet. But the other part—the tired, fraying part—wanted to open it.

Jay's voice came low through the door: "Nia. I know you in there."

He always knew.

She cracked the door.

Jay's gaze locked on her face, sharp and steady. The dim hallway light cut across his features— strong jaw, faint stubble, dark eyes that never missed a thing.

He lifted the bag in his hand with a small   shrug, teasing but laced with concern."Figured you ain't eat."

Nia swallowed, pride pushing her to joke, but exhaustion louder.

She stepped back, letting him in.

Jay set the takeout on the counter, his eyes scanning the apartment.

Concern flickered across his face before he smoothed it over.

"You good?" he asked, casual, but heavy.

Nia crossed her arms tight, drowning in her hoodie.

"You really bring food or just trying invade my space?"

His lips twitched. "Both. You eating', though."

The smell of fried rice and lemon pepper wings filled the room.

But Nia barely noticed. Her chest was tight, her nerves stretched thin.

Jay unpacked the containers like he belonged there,   but his eyes kept cutting back to her— steady, sharp, reading every crack she tried to hide.

She couldn't keep him out forever.

The hum of the AC filled the silence.   The glow from the streetlights sliced broken stripes across the walls.

Nia curled on the couch, arms wrapped around herself.
Jay leaned on the counter, eyes never leaving her.

The food sat untouched.

"You eat today?" he asked. Not small talk.

She shrugged. "I ain't hungry."

"You always hungry."

But tonight, the rhythm was off.

Jay's smirk faded. "You good?"

Simple. Soft. Loaded.

Her pride answered first. "I'm good."

But even to her, it rang false.Jay pushed off the counter, steps soft across the floor.

Her pulse picked up, arms tightening like she could hold herself together.

"You sure?" he asked, crouching low,   steady and close. "You moving'   like you got the whole world sitting' on your chest."

The words cut deep.

Her chin tucked, voice raw. "You ever just… feel like you trying' to hold it all together, but it's falling' apart anyway?"

Jay's eyes stayed on hers, his voice rough but real. "Every damn day."

No judgment. No flinch. Just steady.

Her throat tightened, tears burning.

"I'm fine," she whispered, voice breaking.

Jay's hand lifted, slow, easy, resting gentle on her knee.

"You ain't gotta be fine with me."

The words cracked something wide open.

For the first time all night, Nia let herself breathe.

CHAPTER 03

"Rides & Late Nights"

Morning After

The morning light crept through the blinds,   slicing pale gold stripes across the faded tile floor, the old coffee table,   and the pile of unopened mail   still sitting from last night.

Outside, the block was waking up—the faint grind of an engine turning over, a car door   slamming, the metallic rattle of   a shopping cart   being pushed down the sidewalk. Somewhere down the street,   a dog barked, sharp and impatient.

But in here?

Stillness.

Nia's eyes cracked open,   lashes heavy with a sleep too shallow to ease the coil in her chest. The worn couch creaked faintly beneath her as she stretched, her legs tangled in an over   sized hoodie and the thin throw blanket she barely remembered pulling over herself.

Her body ached with bone-deep exhaustion that   no nap could cure. Her throat was dry, her mouth stale, her temples throbbing. But none of it compared to the dull, heavy ache in her stomach—the one that hadn't left since yesterday.

The test.

The two pink lines.

The truth staring back at her: cold, sharp, undeniable.

Her gaze drifted toward the corner of the room.

Jay. Still here.

He was slumped sideways in the armchair,   long legs stretched out,   arms crossed over his chest, head tilted against   the cushion. His hoodie had ridden up at   the waist, the faint line of ink curling along his side—black script and bold lines peeking out. His face was relaxed, but tension clung even in sleep: his jaw set, his brows faintly furrowed,   his guard never fully down.

The quiet hum of the AC filled the apartment, pushing cool   air that couldn't clear the heaviness in the room. Takeout containers still sat on the counter, the faint smell of fried rice and lemon pepper wings hanging in the air, dull now.

Nia rubbed her eyes, her chest tightening as the weight of   last night crept back in—her walls cracking, Jay's voice steady,   his hand warm on her knee, the way she folded when she had tried so hard to hold it together.

And him— Not judging.

Not pushing.

Just… staying.

She peeled herself from the couch, bare feet brushing the cool   tile as she stood. Shadows wrapped the apartment,   the morning light creeping along the edges. At the fridge, she grabbed a water bottle,   the cold air brushing her arms with goosebumps. She unscrewed the cap, taking slow sips that eased her throat but not the knot in her stomach.

Jay shifted in the chair, brows pinching faintly, like even in sleep some part of him registered the unease.

Nia leaned against the counter, eyes fixed on him—the curve of   his jaw, the faint scruff, the quiet weight of him just being here.

How many nights had they done this?

Late talks. Fries on the couch.   The TV humming.   His steady presence filling her space like it   belonged.But this time the lines weren't   clean. The air wasn't light.

Her hand drifted to her stomach, palm pressing the over sized hoodie. The memory of those two sharp pink lines sat loud behind her ribs. She wasn't ready to tell him. She wasn't even ready to tell herself.

Something was shifting, steady as a train she couldn't outrun.

The creak of the chair broke her spiral.   Jay stirred, eyes cracking open— dark, groggy, landing on her instantly.

For a second, silence. Just the hum of the AC, the buzz of morning outside, the weight of everything unsaid.

He rubbed his eyes, voice rough with sleep.

"You good?"

The same words as last night.

But now? They hit different.

Nia's throat tightened. She forced a faint smirk that didn't reach her eyes.

"Yeah," she lied. "I'm good."

Jay didn't push. But the way his eyes lingered—steady, sharp, quietly reading every fracture— said more than words could.

Tasha Knows

The buzz of fluorescent lights hummed over Nia's head as she stepped behind the counter at Sole Stop. The scuffed tiles creaked beneath her sneakers, the air heavy with rubber, cardboard, and synthetic leather.

The store was quiet—early morning slow. The wall clock ticked deliberate, posters of old sneaker releases hung crooked, and the plexiglass cases fogged from the humidity sneaking through the front door.

Nia slid her bag under the counter, fingers shaky on the zipper, sleeves tugged down over her hands. Her stomach twisted—not from nerves but from reality. The two pink lines followed her in like a shadow.

She grabbed the price gun, its plastic cool in her palm, the faint beep echoing as she worked the display table, motions detached.

"You gone' tell me what's wrong, or you just plan on lying' to my face all day?"
Tasha's voice cut through before she could sink deeper.

Nia froze mid-scan, turning to the back corner.Tasha leaned against stacked shoe boxes, arms folded, acrylics tapping her forearm. Her expression was sharp, unimpressed, and knowing. Long braids framed her face, lashes thick, hoops catching light as she tilted her head—I already know, don't waste my time look only family could master.

Nia sighed, jaw tight. "Ain't nothing' wrong."

"Uh huh." Tasha's nails clicked against the box. "You showing'   up looking' like a damn sleepdeprived ghost,   hoodie swallowing' you, eyes all puffy... you expect me to believe that?"

"I'm just tired, Tasha," Nia snapped, sharper than she meant, her voice fraying at the edges.

Tasha arched a brow, unfazed. "Tired? Or pregnant?"

The word hit like a brick.

Nia's fingers froze, breath hitching.

Tasha's tone softened slightly, though the realness stayed. "I seen the test in your bag, Ni. You can't hide that from me."

Heat rushed to Nia's face. She spun around, arms crossed tight. "You went through my bag?"

Tasha rolled her eyes. "Girl, I ain't got to. You left it wide open, box staring' at me like it had something' to say."

Nia's jaw clenched, her chest pounding. "You tell anybody?"

"Nah," Tasha said, softer now. "Ain't my place."

Silence stretched, filled by the AC hum and faint chatter from outside.

"You tell Jay yet?" she asked finally, sharp again.

Nia looked away, throat tight.

Tasha let out a humorless laugh. "That's a no."

"It's complicated," Nia muttered, voice small.

"It ain't complicated," Tasha shot back. "You pregnant. Marcus ain't shit.

Jay? He already showing' up harder than that boy ever has."

Nia flinched, pride and fear colliding behind her eyes.

Tasha's voice softened but stayed real. "Stop running', Ni. You can't dodge this."

Nia swallowed hard, the silence heavy, her walls cracking one by one.

For now, the truth stayed stuck.

But the clock was ticking.

Another Ride, Another Night

The faint ding of the Sole Stop doorbell   faded as Nia stepped into the sticky night air.

The city hummed—streetlights buzzing, cars rumbling, teens laughing too loud on the corner. Fried food and exhaust tangled heavy in the humidity.

Her feet ached, shoulders tight, exhaustion pressing beneath her hoodie. But it wasn't just work. It was everything.

The test.

The two pink lines.

The words stuck behind her teeth.

And Jay—steady against his Mustang across the street,   posted like the block couldn't move him.

The car gleamed faint   under the streetlights, windows down, engine rumbling low, bass vibrating soft. Jay leaned against the driver's door, shoulders relaxed, ankle crossed, phone loose in hand.

His eyes found her the second she stepped off the curb.

His mouth pulled into that familiar smirk—the one that never tried too hard.

"You look dead."

Nia snorted, lips curving faint. "I feel worse."

He popped the passenger lock with a click. "C'mon. Before you pass out on the sidewalk."

Inside, the Mustang smelled like him—soap, leather, a trace of motor oil.

Nia slid in, cool leather against her thighs. Jay climbed behind the wheel, engine purring as he eased onto the street, one hand on the wheel, the other adjusting the vents.

The city slipped past—traffic thinning, corner stores closing, stragglers drifting under the hum of streetlamps.

Silence stretched, filled by low R&B—smooth vocals, bass steady, the rhythm slow as the block exhaled.

Nia watched the window—the sidewalks, the leaning palms, the boarded laundromat mural.

Their neighborhood, unchanged, heavy with history. Her fingers traced her hoodie seam, thoughts spiraling.

She could tell him.

Right now.

But fear held her still.Jay's hand hovered over the radio. "You trying sit in silence the whole way, or you want the aux?"

Nia snorted, grabbing her phone. "You lucky I ain't torturing' you with my music tonight."

"You been torturing' me for years," he smirked, turning onto their block.

She queued another soft track, mellow bass filling the space.

The car rolled to a stop outside her apartment, engine idling, headlights casting long shadows.

Neither moved.

The music played. The air thickened.

Jay drummed his fingers, jaw tight, eyes flicking her way.

"You sure you good?"

Same words. Same steady patience.

Nia's chest tightened. She wanted to tell   him. About the weight in her stomach. About the fear.

About how he showed up when nobody else did.

But her walls stayed up.

"Yeah," she whispered, voice shaky, paper-thin.

Jay didn't press. But his gaze lingered, peeling her defenses with silence.

The neighborhood carried on—a dog barking,   a door   creaking, tires humming.

Inside the car, time slowed. The space between them shrank.   The line between friends and something more blurred.

But neither crossed it. Not yet.

His gaze drifted back to the wheel.

"Call me when you wake up," he said softly. "If you need anything."

Her throat tightened, but she nodded, slipping out into the heavy night.

The Mustang rumbled as she closed the door,   Jay's eyes following until she disappeared inside.

The words stuck behind her teeth.

But the clock was ticking.

The Missed Call

The door   clicked shut,   the deadbolt   sliding into place with   a quiet scrape.Nia leaned against it, body heavy, heart pounding steady.

The apartment smelled of lavender spray and old takeout—the faint trace of fried rice and lemon pepper still   lingering. The couch sagged beneath her hoodie, the coffee table cluttered with mail,   keys tossed beside a chipped coaster.

Everything looked the same.

But nothing felt the same.

The AC hummed, but it couldn't cool the heat pressing low in her stomach. The two pink lines still sat in the bathroom—sharp, undeniable.

Streetlight shadows stretched jagged across   the floor.   Outside, Jay's Mustang idled, his silhouette faint through the glass. She could feel   him— steady, waiting. Always.

Her phone buzzed against her thigh, sharp in the silence.   She flinched, fumbling. The screen lit.

Marcus.

Her heart sank.

She stared at the name, the old photo—him smirking in a hoodie. Days of silence, and now this.

She answered.

"Hello?" Her voice cracked, rough, guarded.

"Damn, Ni..." Marcus's voice slid through,   smooth, casual, leaning on charm. "I been meaning' to hit you. It's been crazy, you know how it be." Silence stretched. She said nothing.

He chuckled faintly, empty sound landing cold.   "What, you mad at me or something'?"

Her jaw clenched, fingers curling in her hoodie. She held the silence longer.

His tone faltered. "Look, I know I been ghosting' a little. But I'm pull up soon, alright? You been on my mind."

Her throat tightened, eyes burning. On his mind. Funny.

The two pink lines burned behind her eyes, heavier than his words.

"I'm pregnant," she said flat, sharp. No buildup. Just truth.
Silence.

Her heartbeat thundered, AC humming in the background.

Finally: "Wait… for real?"Her lips pressed tight,   voice steady, cold. "For real."

Another pause. Panic leaked behind his tone.   Alright… alright, we gone' figure it out. I'm come by soon, we can talk."

But the hesitation was there. The quiet exit already planned.

She'd heard it all before. Excuses. Promises. Disappearances.

"You ain't got to figure nothing' out," she said low, sharp enough to cut. "I'm good."

He started to protest, but she ended the call.

The screen went black.

The weight pressed harder in her chest. She curled into herself   on the couch, arms wrapping tight around her midsection.

Outside, Jay's car still sat steady by the curb.

He didn't know yet.

But he was here.

And that meant more than Marcus ever could.

CHAPTER 04

"Cracks in the Walls"

The faint click of the door settling back into place echoed softly in the apartment, the old lock sliding into the frame with a quiet finality that made Nia's pulse jump. Jay stood just inside, broad shoulders relaxed, hands loose in the pockets of   his hoodie, eyes drifting over the room— the low light, the sagging couch, the blanket crumpled on the cushion, the silence pressing thick against the air. But his gaze kept landing on her.

Nia hovered by the window, arms wrapped tight around her midsection, hoodie sleeves pulled down over her hands, her whole body wired like a string pulled too far. For a long moment, neither spoke. The hum of the AC filled the space, brushing cool against her skin, but it didn't ease the heat pressing under her hoodie—the nerves, the pressure, the weight of what she wasn't saying.

Jay toed off his sneakers and stepped further in, his voice breaking the quiet, low and steady, carrying that calm only he seemed to have.

"You want me to go?"Nia shook her head before pride could trip her up.

"Nah."

He nodded once, sank into the couch like he'd done a hundred times, and waited. No push, no questions—just steady silence.

Nia paced, bare feet sliding against the cool tile, arms locked around herself, her heart stumbling an uneven rhythm.   Jay's eyes tracked her every step, every twitch, every pause.

"You gone' burn a hole in the floor," he muttered, humor tucked low in his voice.

She shot him a look, the corner of her mouth twitching faint before slipping away again. "Maybe I will," she said, weak but defiant.

Then—"Nia."

The way he said her name shifted the air.   She stopped. His eyes caught hers—sharp, steady, reading her like an open book.

"You wanna say   something', or you want   me to keep sitting'   here guessing'?"
The test. The two pink lines. Marcus's voice—slick and fading. Jay, here, steady, waiting. The words pressed against her lips but stayed stuck, pride clawing tight around her chest. She looked at the floor.

Jay leaned back, softer now. "Say it or don't. I'm here either way."

The silence crept in again—the AC's hum,   the fridge's buzz,   the low city sounds through the cracked window.   Nia rocked on her   heels, pride tangled with fear, walls cracking faint beneath her skin. But the words didn't come. Jay stayed steady.   And she stayed standing,   pride fraying but holding on—barely.

The air thickened. Not with small talk. Not with noise. With tension—hot, heavy, running up her arms and curling in her stomach.   Jay sat stretched on the couch, tattoos catching in the lamplight, gaze locked on her like he could peel her apart without a word.

Nia shifted, her chest tight, her pride falling apart one breath at a time. "You gone' stand over there all night acting' like I bite?" he teased, lips tugging faint.

Her mouth twitched. "I'm thinking' about it," she whispered back.

Something buzzed between them,   louder than the music drifting soft   from her speaker. Nia's legs carried her forward before her mind could second-guess. The floor creaked beneath her as she crossed to the couch and sat—close, too close. Their knees brushed, her pulse hammering.

Jay stayed still,   eyes flicking darker,   softer. The room pressed in—lamp glow, city hush, lavender in the air. She could hear her heartbeat in her ears. His hand rested easy on his thigh, fingers drumming steady.

Her hand lifted, shaky, curling into his hoodie, tugging him the last inch.

The kiss came quiet— careful,   patient. The kind that   spoke for every moment they'd been too stubborn to say it   out loud. His thumb brushed circles against her knee, grounding her.

Whenthey pulled apart,   foreheads resting together,   their breaths tangled. Neither spoke. They didn't need to. It was in the way her fingers clung to him, in the steady press of their knees, in the absence of space between them. The line they'd drawn was gone. Crossed. Forgotten.

Morning crept in slow,   blinds slicing sunlight   across the tile.   The quiet lingered, heavy but different—the kind that hummed against your ribs, that stayed after crossing a line you couldn't take back.

Nia lay curled on the couch,   Jay's warmth pressed against   her back, his arm slung low around her   waist, palm resting light   on her stomach. His breath brushed the back of her neck, chest rising slow against her shoulder blades. The blanket half-slipped to the floor,   the air cool against her skin, her hoodie bunched at her waist. Her heart thudded slow, uneven.

But the loudest thing? The secret sitting sharp beneath her ribs.

The two pink lines burned behind her eyelids, stamped across the walls of the apartment. They weren't going away. And Jay didn't know.

Her throat tightened. Her body tensed faint against him. He stirred, sliding his hand higher, thumb brushing soft against her ribs.

"You up?"   His voice was rough with sleep,   warm, carrying weight   it shouldn't.

She nodded, curls brushing the pillow. His hand lingered.

"You want me to go?"

Her eyes opened.   Sunlight stretched across the coffee table,   catching cracks in the tile,   unopened mail, her phone face down.   She turned just enough to meet his gaze—sleep-heavy but still sharp, steady, reading her like glass.

She shook her head. "No."

His edges softened. The quiet stretched—the hum of the AC, a car outside, a dog barking faint through the walls. But beneath it all, the secret pressed harder, louder.

Her hand drifted beneath the blanket, curling protectively over her stomach, pulse racing beneath her   palm. The words perched on her   tongue—the truth, the weight, the thing that could unravel everything. But they stayed stuck.

Jay searched her eyes, patient, waiting. The sunlight crept across the floor, the city waking outside.   Inside, the truth stayed tangled in her chest.   She swallowed hard, eyes closing again, fingers pressing against her stomach.

And Jay? He stayed. Quiet. Steady. Unknowing. For now.

CHAPTER 05

"The Truth Don't Wait"

The low, steady hum of the AC filled the apartment, the quiet rattle of the old unit pushing cool air that barely touched the heat burning along Nia's skin. The faint hiss of the coffee maker joined the background — water dripping slow, the old machine sputtering faint as steam curled into the still air, mixing with the bitter scent of dark roast and the faint lavender clinging to the apartment walls.

Sunlight crept through the crooked blinds, long stripes of gold slicing across the floor, climbing up the coffee table, catching on the pile of unopened mail and the worn edges of the couch cushions.

Nia sat curled tight on the couch — hoodie sleeves pulled low over her hands, knees tucked beneath her, her bare feet pressing against the cool tile. Her body coiled inward, small, defensive, her shoulders hunched like she could fold into herself and disappear if she held still long enough.

Her eyes stayed locked on the floor — the cracks in the old tile, the faint scuff marks by the baseboards, the tiny chip in the coffee table corner she'd been meaning to fix for months. Anything but Jay. But even without looking, she could feel him — his presence filling the small space, steady, warm, impossible to ignore.

The faint clink of a cabinet opening.

The low scrape of a mug pulled from the shelf.

The soft creak of the counter as he leaned his weight against it.

Normal sounds.

Familiar sounds.

But today? They twisted in her ears, warped by the heavy pulse pounding behind her ribs.

Jay moved around the kitchen like he belonged there — like this morning wasn't different, like last night hadn't blurred every line between them.

Her chest tightened. Her stomach turned. The pregnancy. The test hidden in the bathroom. The weight pressing down harder with every breath.

Jay's voice broke the quiet, low and rough from sleep, cutting through the room without rushing it.

"You want some?" he asked, his tone easy, steady, nodding faint toward the coffee pot.

Nia's throat clenched. Her stomach twisted tighter, nausea creeping up her chest, sharp and hot. She shook her head — small, quick — her lips too dry to speak, her voice tangled behind the knot in her throat.

Jay shrugged, casual, pouring a mug for himself, the faint splash of liquid filling the silence, the scent curling stronger in the air. He leaned against the counter, cradling the mug between his palms, his eyes finally drifting to hers.

Sharp. Steady. Unflinching.

Nia's pulse skipped.

"You good?"

The same question. Simple. Soft. But this time? It slammed into her like a weight to the chest.

The couch felt too small. The apartment felt like it was shrinking around her. The words clawed their way up her throat. The two pink lines burned behind her eyelids — louder than the hum of the AC, louder than the traffic beyond the window, louder than the steady quiet in Jay's voice.

She couldn't lie. Not this time. Not with him still standing there. Still showing up. Still steady when everything else felt like it was cracking apart.

Her fingers clenched tight in the sleeves of her hoodie, her shoulders curling inward, her knees pulling higher to her chest as the weight in her stomach twisted again, sharp and inescapable.

Jay didn't look away. Didn't rush her. Just… waited. Patient. Present. Nia's heart hammered behind her ribs, the sound deafening in her ears, her tongue heavy in her mouth, the truth crawling higher, pressing against her lips.

It wouldn't stay down. Not anymore. Not with him here. Not with the weight in her chest pushing her to the edge.

It was coming. Messy. Raw. Inevitable.

The air in the apartment held still   — thick, unmoved — like the room itself
had frozen in place,   waiting for the next breath, the next word, the next
fracture to spread wide and loud across the silence. Nia's chest squeezed
tight, her ribs aching from the pressure pressed low and sharp inside
her.

Her hands curled tighter in the sleeves of   her hoodie, her fingers twisting
the fabric, pulling at the worn threads like they could hold her   together
when her whole body felt like it was splitting apart.

Across the room,   Jay stood by the counter,   one hand resting against   the
edge, his coffee mug untouched, forgotten now, the steam curling faint into
the air, blending with the stale lavender scent clinging to the walls.

His eyes never left her. Steady.   Watching. Waiting. But the patience in his
stare? It made it worse. Made the weight   press harder. Made the secret
claw its way up her throat faster.

Her pulse pounded behind her   ears, loud and uneven,   drowning out the
faint hum of the AC, the soft gurgle of the old coffee pot,   the distant city
sounds bleeding faint through the window.

Her mouth opened —

Closed —Opened again —

Pride fighting, fear twisting —

But the words broke loose anyway,   raw and jagged,   scraping against her
teeth as they tumbled out.

"I'm pregnant."

The room snapped quiet. The words hung thick in the air, settling between
them like smoke that wouldn't clear.

Jay's eyes stilled — not wide,   not flinching, but sharp, locked on her face,
the unreadable quiet of his expression freezing the air solid.

Nia's heartbeat raced, her lungs tightening,   the pressure under   her ribs
burning hotter as the rest of the words clawed free.

"It's…" She swallowed hard, the name bitter and sharp on her tongue. "It's Marcus's."

The silence that followed wasn't empty. It was full. Full of tension. Full of quiet shock. Full of everything they weren't saying yet.

Jay's jaw tensed faint — the muscle flexing under the soft   line of stubble along his cheek, his mouth pressing tight, his stare locked on hers so still   it made the hairs along her   arms rise. He didn't move. Didn't breathe, it seemed. Didn't speak.

But his eyes — sharp,   heavy, quiet — stayed locked on hers,   tracking every crack forming across her expression, reading her like he always did, peeling back her pride, her defenses, her fear with nothing but patience.

The words sat between them like a weight — real, permanent, inescapable.

Nia's body stayed curled tight,   her knees drawn up,   her arms locking around herself, the oversized hoodie swallowing her small   frame like armor that couldn't hide how small she felt inside it.

Her throat worked hard, the lump lodged behind her tongue burning as she forced herself to keep breathing, keep holding his gaze, even when every instinct screamed to look away.

The AC hummed low. The coffee pot hissed faint. The city outside carried on — but in here? Time didn't move.

She expected him to say something.   Anything. To react — to leave — to break —

But Jay? He just stood there. Still. Steady. His stare heavy, unreadable, cutting through the quiet like it could unravel her all by itself.

And Nia? She sat frozen, her chest tight, her world tilting, the truth hanging in the air so loud she could barely breathe past   it. There was no taking it back now. The secret? It wasn't a secret anymore.

The silence stretched long — thick as the heat   in the room,   loud as the racing of Nia's heartbeat pounding behind her ribs. The words still   hung in the air. Pregnant. Marcus. Final.

Jay hadn't moved. Not a muscle. Not a breath. His hand rested against the counter, his coffee forgotten, the faint steam curling from the mug unnoticed as his eyes stayed locked on her — sharp, steady, unreadable.

Nia sat curled small on the couch, her arms wrapped tight around her knees, her chest tight, her pride frayed and barely holding, her throat raw from forcing the truth out.

Her eyes flicked to his face — tracking every inch — the slight clench in his jaw, the faint crease between his brows, the set of his mouth, pressed tight like he was holding something behind his teeth. She expected the questions. The disappointment. The judgment. Or worse — silence followed by him walking out that door.

But Jay? He didn't move. His stare stayed locked on her — not cold, not angry — just… steady. Present. Patient.

The air in the apartment pressed in heavy — the hum of the AC, the faint buzz of traffic beyond the window, the coffee maker hissing faint in the corner — all of it blurred beneath the weight of the moment sitting loud between them.

Jay's chest rose with a quiet breath, slow, even. His shoulders relaxed just enough to shift his posture, but he didn't speak. Not yet.

The quiet filled the space, but it wasn't empty. It was full. Full of shock. Full of that quiet steadiness he always carried when her world started spinning sideways.

Nia's throat tightened, her eyes burning, her pride shoving hard against the panic climbing up her chest. But her walls? They cracked all over again. Wide. Loud. Unavoidable.

Jay finally pushed off the counter — slow, deliberate — his footsteps light across the tile as he crossed the room.

Nia tensed. Her arms hugged tighter around herself. Her breath hitched. But Jay? He didn't crowd her. Didn't reach for her. He just… sat. Lowered himself onto the couch beside her, his broad frame settling into the cushion, his knees brushing against hers, his hand resting loose on his thigh.

He didn't say anything. But his presence? Louder than words. Solid. Steady. Unshakable.

Nia's eyes flicked to him, wide, rimmed with the threat of tears she couldn't swallow fast enough, her chest aching from holding everything in so long. Jay tilted his head slightly, his eyes softening at the edges — sharp, yes, but warm now — reading every crack in her expression, every breath shaking its way past her lips.

The weight in her throat shattered.

"I didn't... I didn't wanna tell you like that," she whispered, voice breaking soft and raw, her fingers curling into the sleeves of her hoodie. "I just... I couldn't hold it in no more."

Jay's jaw flexed faint, but his voice when it came? Low. Steady. Soft in a way that cracked something wide open in her chest.

"I ain't going' nowhere."

The words hit harder than the silence. Harder than anything else he could've said.

Nia's breath shook, her pride finally collapsing the rest of the way, her arms falling loose from her knees as she curled faint toward him, her body trembling, her chest hollow and raw.

Jay didn't hesitate. His hand lifted — slow, careful — settling warm against her knee, his thumb brushing small, steady circles into the fabric of her hoodie. He didn't press. Didn't crowd. Didn't demand anything from her. He just... stayed.

And for the first time in what felt like forever? Nia let herself lean into him. Let the last of her walls fall all the way down. Let the fear settle, tangled with the steady heat of him beside her.

The truth was out. The future? Still messy. Still heavy. But Jay? He was all the way in now.

The quiet stretched wide across the small apartment — a different quiet now. Not sharp. Not suffocating. Just... still.

The hum of the old AC filled the space, low and steady, pushing faint, cool air that brushed along Nia's skin but couldn't cool the warmth radiating off her cheeks, her chest, the inside of her palms where they pressed against the couch.

The sunlight   leaking through the blinds   had shifted,   creeping longer, warmer, casting soft golden lines across the floor,   up the coffee table, across the faded couch cushions.

Nia sat curled in the corner   of the couch, knees tucked halfway beneath her, her hoodie pulled loose at the collar, her arms limp now — not locked tight around herself, not clenched — just… loose. Exhausted. Exposed.

Jay sat   beside her,   close but   not crowding — his frame leaned back against the couch,   his arm stretched along the back cushion,   his other hand resting loose against his thigh, fingers tapping faint against his jeans.

His eyes? Still locked on her. Still steady. Still reading her like he always did — peeling her apart layer by layer, but this time? She let him.

The words she'd spoken still   lingered heavy in the air,   thick with finality, curling into every corner of the room. Pregnant. Marcus. The raw truth of it all hanging visible now, impossible to swallow back down.

Nia's chest ached under   the weight,   her pulse slowing from its frantic rhythm, but not steady yet. Her pride? Crumbling at her feet. But the fear? It lingered sharp behind her ribs.

She glanced at   Jay again — tracking the line of   his jaw, the faint crease between his brows, the set of his mouth — tight,   quiet, unreadable in that way only he managed.

The questions tangled behind her teeth slipped out softer than she meant, rough and hesitant, her voice cracking faint in the stillness.

"You mad?"

Jay's gaze met hers, steady, holding, no flinch, no shift. His head shook once — slow, deliberate.

"Nah," he said, his voice quiet but solid, the faint rasp of sleep still   roughing the edges. "I'm just… trying sit with it."

Nia nodded faint, her eyes drifting to her   hands where they twisted faint against the couch fabric,   fingers curling in on themselves like they didn't know where to settle.

The weight pressed in again — not crushing, but undeniable — thicker than the humidity curling outside the window, heavier than the tight coil still locked low in her belly.

Her throat tightened, her pride tugging one last time, but her chest eased open as the words cracked loose.

"I ain't expect this," she admitted, her voice small, raw, the edges of it shaky, frayed.

"Any of this."

Jay's arm shifted faint along the couch back, his frame settling heavier into the cushion, his knees brushing hers just enough to feel steady.

"Yeah," he murmured low, his eyes softening, tracking her face like every shift in her expression told him more than words ever could.

"Me neither."

The apartment hummed quiet again — the low whir of the AC, the distant buzz of traffic, a neighbor's TV muffled faint through the wall.

Nia sat with it — the quiet, the fear, the truth sitting loud in her chest, but… shared now.

Not buried.

Not held alone.

Jay's hand drifted slow across the couch, his fingers brushing faint against her knee — not grabbing, not pulling — just there. Steady.

A soft, unspoken anchor in the middle of the unknown.

"I'm here," he said finally, his voice rough around the edges, low but steady enough to sink deep.

"You ain't got to do this alone."

The words cracked through her chest, loosening something sharp behind her ribs, settling warm and heavy beneath the mess of everything else.

Nia nodded once, her hand brushing faint over his, her pride quiet now, her body sinking softer into the couch beside him.

The future? Still   messy. Still heavy. Still full of questions she couldn't answer yet. But for the first time? She didn't   feel like she was carrying it alone.

CHAPTER 06

"Block Talk & Broken Promises"

The buzz of   the block wrapped around them as they stepped onto the corner lot near Rico's— heat   radiating off   the pavement,   the hum of conversations floating low from doorways and porches,   the faint   static crackle of somebody's old radio drifting out of a window overhead. The air smelled like grease, fried fish, and the faint bite of hot concrete baking in the sun.

Jay stayed close at Nia's side—hands buried in his hoodie pockets,   head on a slow swivel,   eyes reading the block the way he always did: calm, sharp, watching for the energy shift before it hit.

But Nia? She could feel   it already. The whispers. The eyes. The weight creeping up her spine. Her palms were damp inside her sleeves, her chest tight, her pulse loud behind her   ears as they moved toward the front   of Rico's.

That's when she spotted the silver Altima pulling up at   the curb, its bass rattling faint   under the beat-up speakers.   The windows were down,   the glitter of acrylic nails catching sunlight   as a familiar   hand tapped against the steering wheel.

Tasha. Perfect timing—or terrible, depending on how you looked at it.

The car barely idled before Tasha threw it in park, her door swinging open with all the quiet subtlety of a hurricane. Long box braids swayed as she stepped out,   gold hoops glinting in the sun,   lashes thick enough to cast their own shadows.   Her whole energy was loud before she even opened her mouth.

Her gaze landed on Nia—sharp, knowing, the kind of look family reserved for when they already had the whole story before you could say a word. Jay slowed his steps, his hand brushing faintly at the small   of Nia's back— not pushing, not holding, just there.

Tasha's hips cocked to the side, arms crossing over her chest, her acrylics tapping against her forearm as she let her eyes sweep from Nia to Jay and back again. Her mouth curled with that   cousin-style amusement dipped heavy in judgment.

"Mm," she hummed, loud enough to cut   across the lot. "Ain't you brave stepping' outside today."

Nia's chest   tightened, pride crawling up her   throat, but there was no dodging it now. She stopped walking,   shifting her weight, arms crossing loose as she met Tasha's stare.

"Morning to you too,"   she muttered,   dry, the block's whispers pressing sharper around her.

Tasha clicked her tongue, her smile spreading slow—teeth bright, kindness absent. "Don't play me, Ni," she shot back, stepping closer. "You already know I ain't here for small talk.

"Jay stayed quiet,   his eyes flicking between them,   reading the room but letting it ride.

Tasha's gaze softened just   enough to flash something cousin-deep— concern buried under   sharp edges. "You gonna' tell me how long you planned to keep ducking' me?" she asked, her voice dipping lower, cutting through the street noise. "Or you waiting' 'til the whole damn block finish filling' me in first?"

Nia's throat worked, her jaw clenched,   the heat under her hoodie suffocating. "I wasn't ducking'," she bit back, weak, the lie brittle, snapping under Tasha's stare.

Tasha stepped closer, her acrylics flicking at Nia's arm, her voice low but unsparing. "You pregnant. Marcus ain't nowhere. And Jay?" Her eyes slid to him, sharp but not surprised. "He steady posted beside you like it's his job."

Nia's chest locked tight, the weight of every word folding over her like heat haze rising off   the pavement. But Jay didn't   flinch. Didn't move. His presence beside her was solid, quiet, steady.

Tasha let her words hang for a beat before her mouth curved again—sharp, knowing. "Ain't nothing' subtle 'round here, Ni. But keep acting' like folks ain't already talking'."

The street hummed faint—cars rolling by,   laughter drifting from down the block, bass thumping
from a passing speaker.   But in this moment? It   was just them. Just the truth. Just the eyes.

And Nia? No more hiding.   No more dodging.   The whole block   was watching now.

The quiet energy shifted before she even saw him.   Nia felt it first—the subtle pause in the rhythm of the street, the dip in conversations, the way attention tilted like folks could sense something messy walking up.

Jay felt it too. His stance straightened faint,   his hand pulling from his hoodie pocket, eyes sharpening as he tracked the ripple rolling through the lot.

Tasha's mouth twitched, her head tilting as she followed the same line of attention, her voice rough with cousin-disapproval.   "Speak of the damn devil."

That's when Nia saw him. Marcus.

He crossed the lot   like he owned it,   shoulders loose, grin lazy, phone tucked in one hand, the other gesturing easy—like he hadn't   just ghosted for days, like this wasn't the same old play. Sunlight caught the gold of his chain, glinting sharp as his eyes skimmed the space, landing on Nia. And staying.

Her stomach twisted sharp, palms damp inside her sleeves, heat crawling higher than the Florida sun.   Marcus's grin widened—smooth, casual—the kind she used to fall for, before the silences, before the weak promises.

Jay stayed still beside her. Quiet. Unreadable. His presence heavy enough to settle over the lot.

Marcus's eyes flicked to Jay for half   a beat—sharp, assessing—then slid right back to Nia.

"Damn, Ni," he called, slick voice carrying. "You really making'   me work for this one."

Her chest squeezed tight, tongue pressed to the roof of her mouth, nerves tangled in a knot. Tasha shifted her weight, arms folding tighter, expression dipped in cousin judgment.

Marcus slowed to a stop a few feet away, head tilted, grin holding. "I been trying' to call you," he added, his tone dipping softer, coated in charm that sounded cheap in the heavy air. "We got stuff to talk about."

Nia's jaw clenched.

Jay didn't move. Didn't speak. But his eyes? Locked. Sharp. Quietly reading Marcus like he'd already mapped the whole play.

The block's weight settled—eyes watching, whispers curling, tension coiling.

Marcus's gaze drifted to Jay again—longer this time—grin twitching sharper. "Ain't you always around?" he tossed out, the words dressed light in humor, undercurrent sharp enough to cut.

Jay's body didn't shift. His hands stayed loose. But his presence? Louder than words.

Marcus turned back to Nia, voice softening like they were still alone. "You really ain't gone' talk to me?"

The words landed heavy, false sweetness wrapped around everything unsaid. Nia's throat tightened, pride flickering, the heat of Jay's presence anchoring her. She didn't answer. Not yet. But the moment wasn't going anywhere.

The sound of Marcus's sneakers scuffing against hot pavement echoed as he finally walked off— steps slow, casual, like he hadn't just stirred every nerve in Nia's chest. The lot held still after he turned the corner—eyes lingering, conversations paused, the air pressing down like the whole neighborhood was holding its breath.

Nia's pulse thrummed tight and fast, her hands curled damp inside her sleeves. Jay stayed planted, broad shoulders relaxed, hands loose—but his stillness was charged, coiled, measuring every sound, every step Marcus left behind.

Tasha let out a low snort, shaking her head. "Same old' Marcus," she muttered, acrylics tapping against her arm. "Still talking' slick. Still full of nothing'."

Nia's throat tightened, pride raw, sting sharp behind her eyes.

Tasha's gaze softened faintly, cousin energy curling beneath her sharp tone. "You good?" she asked, low now—less for show, more for real.

Nia's mouth opened. Closed. Her chest squeezed. The truth pressed at the edges but her voice stayed locked.Jay's hand brushed light at the small   of her back—steady, grounding, pulling her from the edge.

Tasha tracked the movement, eyes cutting quick to Jay—sharp, assessing—before her mouth tugged with reluctant approval.

"Alright then," she muttered, stepping back toward her   car. Her eyes lingered on Nia, heavy with cousin-weight, tone soft but pointed. "But I'm be back in your face, Ni. You know me."

Nia nodded, throat dry, the lump behind her tongue too heavy to swallow.

Tasha slid into her   car, engine rumbling, music bleeding faint   from the speakers as she pulled off slow. Tires crunched over cracked concrete.

The lot emptied in waves—folks turning away,   conversations floating back into place, the weight of the moment easing but never gone.

Nia exhaled, slow and unsteady, her shoulders dropping faint   as the sun burned overhead and the familiar sounds of the block crept back in.

But inside? The weight stayed. The whispers lingered. The storm Marcus carried? Not finished.

Jay's hand stayed at her back—not pushing, not demanding, just there. His eyes locked on hers,   steady, reading every crack in her   expression like always.

"You good?" he asked, soft, simple, layered.

Nia's lips pressed tight, heat burning low behind her ribs, pride cracked and raw. But she leaned faint into his space.

"No," she whispered   finally, rough with honesty she couldn't dodge anymore. "But I will be."

Jay's mouth curved faint—not   a smile, not really—but quiet approval tangled with protectiveness that settled between them.

The block carried on around them. But the storm? Just waiting.

CHAPTER 07

"Pressure from Every Side"

The knock still echoed faint in Nia's ears as the door clicked open, the cool air from the AC sliding past her as she met her mother's eyes.

Brenda Williams stood there — tall, lean, pressed jeans hugging her frame, a sleeveless blouse crisp against her skin, her curls slicked back tight into a low bun. Her gold hoop earrings caught the faint overhead light, but it was her eyes — sharp, lined with exhaustion and quiet disappointment — that cut the deepest.

Marcus's eyes flicked to Jay for half a beat—sharp, assessing—then slid right back to Nia. "Damn, Ni," he called, slick voice carrying. "You really making' me work for this one."

Her chest squeezed tight, tongue pressed to the roof of her mouth, nerves tangled in a knot. Tasha shifted her weight, arms folding tighter, expression dipped in cousin judgment.

Marcus slowed to a stop a few feet away, head tilted, grin holding. "I been trying' to call you," he added, his tone dipping softer, coated in charm that sounded cheap in the heavy air. "We got stuff to talk about."

Nia's jaw clenched.

Jay didn't move. Didn't speak. But his eyes? Locked. Sharp. Quietly reading Marcus like he'd already mapped the whole play.

The block's weight settled—eyes watching, whispers curling, tension coiling.

Marcus's gaze drifted to Jay again—longer this time—grin twitching sharper. "Ain't you always around?" he tossed out, the words dressed light in humor, undercurrent sharp enough to cut.

Jay's body didn't shift. His hands stayed loose. But his presence? Louder than words.

Marcus turned back to Nia, voice softening like they were still alone. "You really ain't gone' talk to me?"

The words landed heavy, false sweetness wrapped around everything unsaid. Nia's throat tightened, pride flickering, the heat of Jay's presence anchoring her. She didn't answer. Not yet. But the moment wasn't going anywhere.

The sound of Marcus's sneakers scuffing against hot pavement echoed as he finally walked off— steps slow, casual, like he hadn't just stirred every nerve in Nia's chest. The lot held still after he turned the corner—eyes lingering, conversations paused, the air pressing down like the whole neighborhood was holding its breath.

Nia's pulse thrummed tight and fast, her hands curled damp inside her sleeves. Jay stayed planted, broad shoulders relaxed, hands loose—but his stillness was charged, coiled, measuring every sound, every step Marcus left behind.

Tasha let out a low snort, shaking her head. "Same old' Marcus," she muttered, acrylics tapping against her arm. "Still talking' slick. Still full of nothing'."

Nia's throat tightened, pride raw, sting sharp behind her eyes.

Tasha's gaze softened faintly, cousin energy curling beneath her sharp tone. "You good?" she asked, low now—less for show, more for real.

Nia's mouth opened. Closed. Her chest squeezed. The truth pressed at the edges but her voice stayed locked.

For a second, Nia just stood there, the door half-open, her heart pounding in her chest, the heat behind her ears prickling sharp. Brenda's gaze dropped to the crack in the door, then back to Nia's face — unimpressed, unreadable.

"Open this door, Nia."

Her voice was quiet.

But heavy.

Firm.

No arguing.

Nia exhaled slow through her nose, her pride brittle in her chest as she pulled the door wider, stepping back just enough for her mom to cross the threshold.

The apartment felt smaller instantly — the familiar scent of lavender air freshener and old takeout mixing with the faint citrus of Brenda's perfume, the quiet   tension crackling like static against   the walls.   Brenda's eyes swept the space — sharp,   cataloging — the sagging couch cushions,   the scattered mail on the coffee table,   the faint creak of the old fan rattling on its stand. Then her gaze landed on Jay.

He sat at the edge of   the couch,   elbows resting on his knees,   frame relaxed but steady, dark eyes watching, tracking, reading the whole room with practiced quiet.   Brenda's stare lingered.   Not long. But long enough. Assessing. Weighing.

Jay didn't flinch. Didn't move. Didn't speak.

Brenda's attention slid back to Nia,   her expression pulling tight   with that same quiet command she'd carried Nia's whole life.

"We gonna' talk," she said flat,   her voice low but   layered with everything unsaid.

Nia's throat tightened, her feet carrying her back toward the couch without thinking, her pride trailing like loose threads behind her. She sank onto the cushion beside Jay,   her arms curling faint   around herself, hoodie sleeves tugged low over her palms.

Brenda lowered herself   into the old chair across from them — the faded fabric creaking under   her weight as she sat,   her back straight,   hands clasped loose over one knee. The silence dragged long — heavy — as her eyes settled on Nia, reading every crack in her face like a map.

The hum of the AC filled the room,   faint and steady. The buzz of the city outside bled in — muffled, distant. But in here? The air didn't move.

Brenda's eyes stayed locked on hers — steady,   quiet — but it was her voice, when it finally came, that hit the hardest.

"You pregnant."

Not a question.

A statement.

Final.

Nia's chest squeezed tight,   her lungs fighting to pull   in air past the knot climbing her throat.

"Yeah," Nia forced out, the word cracking at the edges, rough from everything she'd been carrying.
.

Brenda nodded once — slow, deliberate — the tight line of her jaw flexing faint, the crease between her brows pulling deeper.

"And Marcus?" she asked next, the name laced in quiet disapproval, her gaze narrowing faint.

Nia's eyes dropped to her hands — fingers fidgeting in her sleeves, palms damp — her pride cracking wide as she shook her head, voice low, raw.

"He… ain't really been around," she admitted, the ache in her chest pressing harder.

Brenda's exhale was sharp — low but heavy — her head tilting faint as she leaned forward, hands resting light on her knees.

"You letting' him run off again," she said, words sharp but layered with exhaustion,
disappointment folded into every syllable. "And you stuck dealing' with the pieces."

Nia's jaw clenched, her eyes stinging faint, her pride roaring quiet in her chest even as it cracked apart. Jay stayed quiet beside her — unmoved, steady — his presence a quiet wall between her and the weight pressing in from all sides.

Brenda's eyes slid to him again — sharp, reading — her gaze lingering long this time.

"You the new piece?" she asked, her tone pointed, cool, but not cruel — just real.

Jay's stare met hers — solid, unflinching — the corner of his mouth curving faint, not with arrogance, but with steady calm.

"I'm here," he answered, voice low, even, carrying weight without raising the volume.

Brenda's eyes narrowed a fraction — reading him, weighing him — before her attention settled back on Nia.

"You always been stubborn," she muttered, her voice softening faint around the edges, worn with tired love. "But don't let pride drown you."

The words landed hard. Heavy. Final.

The quiet held in the room, layered with tension, with family history, with the storm still brewing beyond the apartment walls.

And Nia?

Pride frayed.

Walls cracking.

But still standing.

Jay?

Still here.

Quiet.

Steady.

Unshaken.

The conversation wasn't done. The pressure? Only building.

The knock barely landed — soft, two taps, more suggestion than demand — but Nia's whole body went   tight. Her pulse skipped. Her grip on the grocery bag clenched faint. The hum of the AC suddenly loud in the quiet apartment.

Jay's head lifted from the couch, his eyes locking on hers — sharp, steady, saying everything without opening his mouth. The walls of the apartment seemed to shift, pressing closer as Nia crossed the space — slow, cautious — her socks brushing soft over the cool tile floor.

The weight in her chest twisted tight. She already knew. Before she even touched the door handle. Before she cracked it open.

Marcus.

Leaning against the door frame like he was right   where he belonged,   one shoulder dipped, hoodie sleeves pushed up to his elbows, the familiar gold chain glinting under   the faint porch light.   In his hand? A bouquet   of gas station flowers — drooping at the edges, wrapped in crinkling plastic, the faint bar code sticker still clinging to the side.

And on his face? That smile. Lazy. Slick. Frayed around the edges, but still performing.

"Damn, Ni," Marcus murmured, voice low, laced with that practiced charm she used to fall for. "You harder to track down than the mailman."

Nia's stomach flipped.   Her fingers tensed around the edge of   the door, breath sticking sharp behind her ribs. She didn't respond — not yet.

Marcus's eyes slipped past   her shoulder, inside the apartment   — sharp, quick — landing on Jay.   His expression faltered.   Just for a second.   But it was enough.

The air thickened. Jay didn't move. Didn't speak. Just sat — elbows on his knees, frame relaxed but   ready, eyes steady, tracking every beat of the moment like a chessboard laid out in front of him.

Marcus pulled his focus back to Nia — his grin returning,   smoother now, forced polish layered over bruised pride.

"I been trying call you," he said, lifting the flowers faint between them, the plastic wrap crinkling sharp in the quiet air. "Just... been a lot going' on.

"Nia's eyes drifted down to the bouquet   — wilting petals,   half-smashed plastic wrapping, price tag still curling at the edges. The weight in her chest pressed harder.

"You good?" Marcus asked, his voice softer   now, manufactured concern curling at the edges.

Nia stayed in the doorway — unmoved,   pride and nerves tangling tight   in her chest.

Marcus's eyes flicked back toward Jay — longer   this time, reading the room, reading the steady quiet that had settled around her apartment.

"You got company, huh?" Marcus tossed out, his grin sharpening just a little, humor layered faint under the words, but the undercurrent? It carried. Heavy. Territorial.

Jay stayed quiet. Didn't shift. Didn't flinch. But his presence? Loud enough to shake the walls.

Nia's pride cracked wide — her hand pressing firm to the door, her voice rough, raw at the edges.

"Nah," she said, steady enough to make herself believe it. "Not tonight."

Marcus's jaw flexed — pride bruised — but his expression smoothed fast, weak grin sliding back into place.

"Alright" he muttered, placing the flowers on the step, his gaze lingering longer than it should've. "You know where I'm at."

His footsteps faded down the walkway — slow, casual — but the tension? It stayed. Thick. Heavy. Loud as hell in the quiet of the apartment.

Nia closed the door — slow, deliberate — the soft click of the lock settling heavy under her ribs as she leaned faint against the wood. Her eyes met Jay's across the room — steady, unreadable — but the unspoken weight in the air? It wrapped around them both now.

The flowers stayed on the step. But Marcus? He wasn't done.

The front door clicked soft behind them, the worn metal screen door bouncing faint against its frame as Nia and Jay stepped out onto the small, cracked stoop.

The air hit heavy. Thick, muggy, hot. The kind of summer heat that pressed into your clothes, sat heavy on your chest, curled tight behind your ears. It clung to Nia's skin instantly — her hoodie suffocating under the sun, the humidity turning her curls heavier, her pulse already tapping wild behind her ribs.

Jay stood beside her — broad shoulders relaxed under the weight of his hoodie, eyes drifting slow across the street, reading the block like it was a language only he understood.

Nia's eyes stayed low at   first — tracking the uneven sidewalk,   the faded chalk lines from somebody's kids,   the cigarette butts ground into the concrete. But she could feel it. The shift. The block breathing down their necks.

They hadn't even hit the curb yet.

Across the street,   old Mr.   Curtis was   sweeping his   porch — slow, deliberate — his eyes following them without   breaking his rhythm. A little farther down, the teenagers by the basketball court paused, their conversation dipping to low murmurs,   eyes cutting toward Nia and Jay, sharp, amused, curious.

The corner   store door   creaked open,   the bell   jingling soft   as someone stepped out   — their gaze catching on them,   lingering a second too long before sliding away.

The whispers curled in the air, faint but sharp.

"She really—"

"Whole block already know—"

"Marcus been sliding' through—"

"Jay ain't left her side though—"

Nia's stomach coiled tight, judgment pressing down on her shoulders,   the heat prickling under   her hoodie like a second layer   of skin. Her heart thudded fast — uneven — shame, fear, pride all tangling behind her ribs.

Jay's shoulder brushed faint against hers as they moved — his hand lifting to press light at the small of her back, a quiet anchor beneath the noise.

"You good?" His voice stayed low, steady, close enough to cut through the buzz crawling under her skin.

Nia swallowed hard,   her throat dry, her eyes darting over   the faces lingering on the block — sharp, curious, quiet.

"Yeah," she muttered, but the lie fractured at   the edges, brittle, ready to splinter.

The smell of grease and car exhaust drifted faint from Rico's down the street, bass from a passing car rattling soft under their feet as they walked. Nia's steps stayed steady on the outside — but inside? Every nerve burned hot. The whispers curled tighter. The block's eyes never left.

By the time they reached the corner, her whole body was wired tight, the weight of every glance, every unspoken word dragging behind her like chains. Jay never flinched. Never spoke. Just stayed close. His body solid beside hers. His presence quiet but louder than any whisper.

The block was watching. But Nia? She wasn't walking through it alone anymore.

The door clicked soft behind them, the faint hum of the AC filling the quiet like static in the heavy air. Nia's back pressed faint against the cool kitchen counter, her fingers curling at the edge, her pulse pounding thick behind her ribs.

Jay stayed by the door — his frame relaxed, but his eyes? Locked on her. Unblinking. Reading every inch of her face like it held the answer to questions neither of them had dared ask yet.

The apartment was quiet — too quiet — the silence stretched tight like a rubber band ready to snap. Outside, the block buzzed faint — distant music, tires crunching over loose gravel, the low hum of conversation — but in here? Time crawled. The air barely moved.

Nia's chest rose and fell — slow, uneven — pride sitting sharp in her throat, nerves crawling under her skin. Jay's eyes tracked her like a slow drag of heat, lingering at the curve of her jaw, the tension in her shoulders, the fingers clenched faint in the fabric of her hoodie.

His voice cut through the silence — low, rough, steady.

"You gonna' keep running'?"

Nia's stomach flipped. Her pride flared for half a second. But her body? Already softening.

She straightened, her shoulder brushing faint against the edge of the fridge, her eyes narrowing just enough to hide how raw her chest felt.

"I ain't running'," she bit back, but her voice cracked quiet at the edges, giving her away.

Jay's mouth curved faint — not a smile, not quite — but the quiet, patient kind of amusement that always saw straight through her defenses.

"You sure?"

Soft.

Simple.

But heavy.

Nia's gaze flicked to his, her heart hammering harder, her walls trembling like glass about to shatter.

Jay pushed off the door slow — each step measured, careful — closing the distance inch by inch, his presence filling the space like heat   rolling under her skin. The apartment shrank around them — the kitchen walls, the faint hum of the fridge, the sound of her own breath catching in her throat.

Jay stopped in front of her — close, but not crowding — his height dipping just enough so their faces aligned, his eyes searching hers like the answer was tangled somewhere in the fear and pride and raw nerves sitting behind them.

Nia's hand hovered at   his hoodie — uncertain — her pulse thudding wild behind her ribs, her body leaning in before her mind could catch up.

Jay's hand lifted slow,   steady — the backs of   his knuckles brushing soft against her jaw, his thumb tracing the curve of   her cheek, his touch light, grounding, impossible to ignore.

"You good?" Same words.

Different now.

Low. Loaded. Heavy with everything they weren't saying.

Nia's eyes slipped closed for half   a breath — chest   tightening, defenses crumbling one crack at a time. Then her hand found his hoodie — fingers curling tight in the fabric — pulling him down the last inch.

The kiss didn't explode.

It wasn't rushed.

It unfolded slow.

Messy.

Heavy.

Jay's mouth pressed soft to hers — careful, steady — his hand sliding to the small of her back, anchoring her, grounding her in the moment.

Nia's pride melted under the heat curling low in her belly — her nerves unraveling as her body eased into his like it had been fighting to for weeks. The air around them pulsed — thick with tension, with fear, with everything that had been simmering too long.

Jay didn't rush it. Didn't push. He let her come to him. Let her fall into the moment — raw, real, no more lines between them.

Her other hand drifted to his chest, the steady rhythm of his heartbeat solid beneath her palm, grounding her, steadying her as her pride cracked wide and her walls crumbled the rest of the way.

The kiss deepened — slow, tangled — the weight of it pressing sharp into the quiet, shifting the air between them for good.

When they finally pulled apart, their foreheads rested together, breaths tangled in the heavy silence, the weight of what they'd done — what they couldn't undo — pressing between them.

Nia's eyes stayed closed, her chest rising slow, pride bruised but forgotten in the heat curling under her skin. Jay's hand lingered at her waist, his thumb tracing faint circles into the fabric of her hoodie, his breath brushing soft across her cheek.

The line? Gone.

Crossed. Left behind in the space they used to pretend was safe.

And now? Everything changed.

CHAPTER 08

"We In This Now"

The soft hum of the old AC filled the apartment   — steady, low, vibrating through the floor and the worn frame of the couch, a faint mechanical   buzz layered under   the quiet.   The blinds shifted faintly in the early morning breeze sneaking through the cracked window,   strips of sunlight creeping across the carpet,   climbing slow along the legs of   the coffee table,   the dusty edges of a pile of unopened mail.

Nia's body stayed still — her eyes half-closed, her breath slow, uneven — but her heart? Pounding. Steady. Heavy.

Jay's arm draped across her waist,   warm and solid,   his hand resting just beneath the curve of her ribs, thumb brushing absent circles into the fabric of her hoodie. His hoodie. It still carried the faint scent of him — detergent, a hint of cologne, the grounding warmth of his skin.

The blanket they'd thrown over themselves sometime after the kiss — after the tension cracked wide open — pooled heavy around their legs,   rough against her bare calves. Her fingers curled at   her side, caught between fear and the slow burn of warmth curling under her skin.

Jay's chest pressed soft to her back, the rise and fall of his breath brushing her spine, the faint scrape of stubble ghosting at the nape of her neck. The moment stretched — long, still, laced with everything they weren't saying.

Outside, the city stirred faintly — muffled traffic, the screech of a bus brake, a radio crackling through some window across the street.   But in here, the world stayed small. Still. Tangled between them.

Jay shifted, his hand sliding at   her waist, fingers curling faintly.   His voice cut quiet into the hush. "You up?"

Low.

Rough with sleep.

Careful.

Nia's throat tightened, pride clawing faint   under her ribs, nerves twisting tight — but her body was already leaning in, already softening into the heat of him. She nodded,   small, cautious, the blanket   rustling low with the movement.

His thumb traced another circle against her side. "You good?"

Same question. Heavier now. Laced with what they couldn't unsay.

She stayed quiet, chest tight, breath catching faint in her throat. But Jay didn't push. Didn't crowd. Just stayed. Steady. Patient. Unshaken.

The quiet filled the room — AC humming low, the soft buzz of the street, the faint creak of a door two floors up. Nia's hand drifted, brushing his arm, the rhythm of his breathing grounding her just enough to exhale. The bubble almost felt safe. Almost.

Then the sharp buzz of her phone cut through the quiet, vibrating hard against the chipped wood of the coffee table.

Nia's body tensed, pulse spiking, eyes snapping open to the glowing screen.

Mom.

The letters burned bright in the shadows, sharp as the ache climbing her throat. Jay's hand eased from her waist, his body pulling back faintly, giving her space, eyes already reading the fear flashing across her face.

The phone buzzed again — louder, sharper — slicing straight through the fragile quiet they'd built. The warmth of Jay's arm, the comfort of the hoodie, the softness of the blanket — all of it cracked under the weight of what waited outside these walls. The real world was here. The morning after ain't never quiet.

The phone buzzed one last time and went still. Silence dropped heavy. Nia sat up, blanket sliding off her legs, hoodie clinging to her skin. Jay shifted too — steady, quiet, his presence filling the space.

The next buzz wasn't a call. It was a text:

Mama: I'm outside. Open the door.

Her breath caught. Eyes snapped to the door. Jay clocked it — the nerves crawling fast up her spine — his shoulders squaring faint as he stood. A knock followed, soft but sharp, three taps that landed like a warning.

Nia's legs carried her before pride could stop her. She cracked the door open.

Brenda Williams stood there. Pressed jeans. Fitted top. Curls slicked back into a tight bun. Gold hoops catching the faint morning light. But it was her eyes — steady, sharp, unreadable — that hit hardest.

Her gaze dropped to Nia's face, then over her shoulder, landing on Jay a few feet back. Hoodie still on, posture easy but unreadable. Her eyes flicked back to Nia.

"Open the door, Nia."

Soft. Firm. Final.

Nia stepped back, throat tight, as Brenda crossed the threshold. Her presence filled the apartment heavier than the summer heat. Jay stayed still, sharp eyes tracking, steady as ever.

Brenda scanned the room — the blanket tossed on the couch, the half-empty water bottle, the creases in the hoodie clinging to Nia. Her expression tightened. Not with anger. Not yet. But with disappointment.

Nia's stomach twisted. Her chest burned. Brenda crossed her arms, eyes locking on her daughter. "We gonna' talk."

Jay didn't move. Didn't interrupt. Just posted, protective without a word. The tension pressed in thick. No dodging now.

Later, when the door finally clicked shut behind them, the air outside felt heavier than inside. Humidity wrapped tight, tension sitting thick. Jay fell into step beside her, sleeves pushed to his elbows, hands in his pockets, scanning the block with practiced ease.

The sun sat high now, Florida heat pressing down. But it wasn't the heat that made her chest tighten. It was the rhythm shift.

Old heads at the corner store paused mid-conversation, eyes drifting. Teens at the basketball court stopped dribbling, murmurs curling low. Mrs. Carter sat on her porch with her plastic fan, eyes tracking like she already knew the storm was near.

And then Nia saw him.

Marcus.

Leaning against a faded blue Altima, chain flashing in the sun, sleeves bunched at his elbows. Grin lazy. But his eyes? Sharp. Tired. Bruised with ego.

He looked at Nia first, then at Jay. The grin stayed, but the energy shifted quick. Heavy.

Jay stayed loose, relaxed, but undercurrent tense. Watching. Ready.

Marcus straightened, crossing slow. Voice slick.

"Damn, you always moving' as a package deal now?"

Dressed in humor. Undercut sharp.

Nia's stomach coiled, pride raw, hand curling in her hoodie. Jay didn't bite. Just watched.

Marcus slid his focus back to her. Voice softening, apology layered like cheap cologne. "I been trying talk to you. Ain't trying to be the bad guy."

The words hung messy, full of everything he wouldn't say out loud. Nia stayed quiet. The block buzzed louder. Jay stayed steady.

When Marcus finally turned and walked off, chain glinting in the sun, the shift came fast. The block spoke now. Not whispers — words.

"That's him…"

"Been posted with her for weeks…"

"Marcus out here looking' real dumb…"

"Whole mess on display…"

Eyes lingered. Mouths moved. Nia's throat tightened, nerves crawling sharp under her skin.

She kept her gaze on the sidewalk, cracks in the concrete, chalk drawings fading on the curb. But the block didn't miss a thing.

Jay brushed her back, light and steady. Quiet anchor. Silent shield.

They turned the corner past Rico's, fried food heavy in the air. More stares. More talk.

"Nia stay posted under him now…"

"Marcus ain't done…"

"Bet it's gonna' blow soon…"

Her chest ached. Pride frayed. Fear pressed in. But Jay stayed beside her. Steady. Carrying the weight without flinching.

The block could whisper.

Could talk.

Could watch.

But for once, she wasn't facing it alone.

CHAPTER 09

"The Breaking Point"

The heat pressed down heavy as they stepped onto the lot   — sunlight creeping high, the concrete warm beneath their shoes, the faint buzz of the city floating low over the block. But the air? It was thicker than just heat. It was heavy with eyes, with whispers, with the weight of what was creeping up behind them.

Jay stayed steady beside Nia — hoodie sleeves pushed up,   broad frame relaxed but eyes sharp, tracking every subtle shift   in the energy around them. Nia felt it too — the pause in conversation as they passed,   the sideways glances, the low hum of words curling sharp under folks' breath. And then she saw him.

Marcus.

Leaning on the hood of his car parked across the lot,   chain heavy against his chest, hoodie sleeves bunched at   his elbows, grin lazy but   sharp, layered with tension so clear it   made the air buzz. His eyes locked on her first — slow, lingering — sliding over   her frame, the pride in his jaw tightening faint before his expression smoothed fast   into that same slick charm she'd once fallen for.

But this wasn't charm. This was bruised ego. A storm building slow behind his teeth.

His gaze flicked to Jay next   — sharp, assessing — the grin widening just enough to show teeth. "Damn, Ni," Marcus called, his voice carrying easy across the lot, coated in humor but cracking at the edges. "You walking' the whole city with your bodyguard now?"

Jay didn't flinch. Didn't move. But his eyes stayed locked,   steady, quietly reading every inch of Marcus.

Nia's pulse tapped fast behind her ribs, her pride tightening under her skin, her hands curling faint inside the sleeves of her hoodie. Marcus pushed off the car — his steps measured,   slow, cutting across the lot   like he owned the space, the block buzzing low behind him.

CHAPTER 10

"The Block Don't Sleep"

The sun burned low in the sky, creeping toward early evening, casting the cracked pavement in soft gold and stretching long shadows across the lot. The heat hadn't gone anywhere—still thick in the air, pressing faint sweat along the back of Nia's neck as she stepped off the stoop, hoodie sleeves bunched at her elbows, nerves coiled tight beneath her skin.

Jay fell into step beside her, broad shoulders relaxed, hands tucked in his pockets, his presence solid and steady, loud without saying a word. But the block? Already clocked them. Already whispering.

A group of old heads near the corner store paused mid-conversation, eyes cutting to them and lingering long, the hum of their voices dipping low. Teenagers by the basketball court bounced the ball slower, their chatter quieting as they passed, curious stares trailing behind them like shadows. The screen door on Mrs. Carter's porch creaked faintly, her sharp eyes following their steps, the old plastic fan clicking soft behind her.

The whispers curled through the air, faint but sharp, heavy.

That's them…

Jay still posted…

Marcus out here talking…

Nia? She really wit' him now…

Nia's pulse tapped fast behind her ribs, pride raw under her skin, the weight of eyes pressing up her back. Jay's hand brushed faintly at her lower back—not pushing, not rushing—just steady. A quiet anchor. Loud in its stillness.

They moved down the block, steps slow, every glance heavy, the buzz of the neighborhood pressing in. Old Mr. Curtis leaned on his porch rail, eyes tracking them, cigarette smoke curling into the hot   air, his expression unreadable. A car rolled past, bass thumping low, windows down, the driver's eyes lingering, sharp, curious. The concrete beneath their shoes was cracked, weeds pushing through the gaps, sidewalks stained with old paint, old chalk, old conversations.

But today? It all felt new. Exposed. Loud.

Nia kept her chin up, her steps steady, but inside pride twisted, nerves tangled, the weight of being seen pressing in. Jay stayed right beside her—quiet, calm—his eyes reading every shift, every whisper, his presence loud enough to ease the sting crawling under her skin. The block didn't sleep. But neither did they. And they weren't hiding anymore.

The block quieted like it felt him coming. Conversations dipped. Basketballs stopped bouncing. Even the birds fell silent for half a second as Marcus stepped out of his car and posted up on the far side of the lot. Arms crossed. Chain glinting. A grin stretched across his face, but it didn't touch his eyes.

Those eyes? Locked dead on Nia. Sharp. Burning. Dripping with bruised pride and ego ready to spill all over the concrete. Jay noticed too—his whole frame still, broad shoulders square, eyes cold and steady, locked in on every shift, every word about to fall from Marcus' mouth.

Marcus dragged his gaze from Nia to Jay—slow, like he was counting steps in his head—then back to Nia.

"Cute," Marcus called, his voice loud enough for the porch ladies, the corner store heads, everybody to hear. "Whole damn neighborhood watching you swap me out."

The air tightened. Side-eyes. Whispers crawling through the lot like smoke.

Nia's stomach flipped, heat crawling up her neck, her hands curling tight at her sides. Jay didn't blink. Didn't shift. But his presence was loud as hell without a single word.

Marcus stepped closer, chest puffed, that lazy grin pulling sharp at the corners now, slick with arrogance but shaky underneath. "You moving funny," Marcus continued, his eyes narrowing faintly, anger creeping beneath the fake charm. "Whole city talking. You got me out here looking like a fool."

Jay's hand slid to Nia's back, slow and controlled, his thumb pressing light against the fabric of her hoodie, anchoring her, steady as a heartbeat.

Nia clenched her jaw, pride burning, pulse racing, the weight of eyes crawling across her skin. Marcus' grin curled sharper, leaning in like he was telling a secret, though the whole block heard every damn word.

"You got my kid," he added, low but coated in venom. "And now you playing house with him?" He tilted his chin toward Jay—mocking, messy, reckless.

The air snapped tight. Even the old heads at the corner store stopped pretending they weren't listening. Jay's stare never wavered—cool, sharp, dangerous in the quietest way.

"I ain't playing at nothing," Jay fired back, voice low, steady, no extra energy—just facts. "I'm here."

Marcus' jaw flexed, the smooth face card cracking, his pride bleeding all over the street.

"You here," Marcus echoed, laughing under his breath, brittle as glass. "Yeah, alright. You steady now. Let's see how long that last when this gets ugly."

Jay didn't move. Didn't flinch. Just let the words hang in the air, heavy as the heat, sharp as a blade.

Nia's heart pounded, pride fraying, nerves twisting. But Jay? Still steady. Still posted. Still saying without saying—he wasn't going anywhere. Marcus backed off, steps slow, cocky, but the tension in his shoulders loud enough to read.

The block was watching like it was a damn movie. Whispers buzzing. Eyes tracking. And Nia? Caught dead center. But for once, she wasn't standing alone.

The front door clicked shut behind them—soft, but the tension still rattled through the house like it never left. The smell of frying chicken lingered in the air, mixing with the faint scent of bleach from the kitchen floor and the old lavender air freshener hanging by the window. But none of it could cover the sharp weight of eyes locked on them the second they stepped in.

Brenda stood by the counter, arms crossed, eyes sharp, the tired edge of disappointment sitting low behind her stare.

Kia and Keisha were still at the table, cups of sweet tea in hand, mouths ready, eyes gleaming with cousin-curiosity and judgment both. The TV in the living room played low, the hum of a news anchor drowned under the thick quiet stretching across the space.

Jay slid in behind Nia, broad frame solid, hoodie sleeves bunched at his elbows, presence steady and loud in that quiet way. Brenda's gaze drifted to Jay, then back to Nia, her mouth pulling tight.

"You gonna' tell me how long this been happening'," Brenda said—not a question, not even loud —just steady, cutting sharper than any yell would have.

Nia's pride prickled raw, her hands twitching faintly at her sides, nerves crawling under her skin.

Kia smirked, leaning back in her chair, nails tapping slow on the tabletop. "Whole block talking' before you even get in the house," she tossed out, her voice light but sharp. "Marcus acting' like he ready to square up. You got this—" she nodded at Jay, "—posted up like security."

Keisha sipped her tea, eyes locked on Jay, amusement curling faint at the corners of her mouth. "I mean, long as you steady…" she murmured, eyes sliding to Nia, tone cutting quiet. "But steady don't always last.

"Brenda's exhale was sharp, jaw flexing faintly as her attention settled heavy on Nia. "I raised you to stand," she said, her voice layered with tired love and sharp pride. "Not lean on the first man who catch you in a mess."

The words landed low in Nia's chest, bruising her pride, twisting behind her ribs. Jay didn't move—didn't flinch—but his hand brushed faintly at the small of her back, anchoring her, solid and quiet.

Nia's mouth opened. Closed. Her heart pounded, nerves knotted tight. But her body? Already leaning toward him. Already done pretending like she didn't need him there.

The silence stretched long. The smell of food. The hum of the TV. The weight of old wounds hanging thick in the air.

Jay's voice broke it—low, respectful, steady. "I ain't here for games," he said, eyes locked on Brenda, calm but heavy. "I'm here 'cause she mine. And I ain't leaving' her in this alone."

The words cracked through the room—sharp, final. The cousins glanced at each other, Brenda's stare holding Jay's for a beat longer than comfort allowed.

The room stayed quiet. Tense. But the wall? Starting to splinter. They weren't folding. Not this time.

The bass from the speakers slid low and heavy over the lot, thumping through sneakers, rattling old porch railings, vibrating in Nia's chest like a second heartbeat. The sun dipped slow, sky melting into orange, pink, and gold, but the heat still clung sticky, rolling down the back of her neck, soaking into her hoodie sleeves.

The lot stretched wide—folding tables sagging with pans of baked beans, foil-wrapped chicken wings, and store-brand sodas drowning in cooler ice. Old men slapped dominoes down on plastic tables, their laughter loud, their eyes sharper, always watching.

Kids weaved through chair legs, sneakers smacking pavement, chalk sketches crawling up curb edges. But the grown folks? Their eyes weren't on the kids. They weren't on the food. They were on Nia and Jay.

The second they stepped onto the lot, the air shifted. Jay moved steady beside her—broad, hoodie sleeves pushed up, chain tucked, jaw set easy—but his eyes? Sharp. Clocking everything. Every side-eye. Every pause in conversation. Every whisper tucked low.

Nia's heart tapped fast, uneven, behind her ribs, but her chin stayed high, her steps steady, even with nerves crawling under her hoodie.

Mrs. Carter sat fanning herself on her porch, foam slippers on, plastic fan whirring slow, eyes tracking them over the rim of her dollar-store sunglasses like she'd been waiting for this.

You see 'them?

They really walking' up like that?

Jay bold, ain't he?And Marcus? I heard he tight tight—

The whispers slid under the smoke rolling off grills, threading beneath the bass line of old-school classics spilling from cheap speakers.

Backstabbers… Smiling' in your face…

Couldn't make this up if they tried.

Nia's hands curled faint at her sides, hoodie sleeves twisting tight between her fingers, pride prickling sharp against her skin. Jay's hand hovered near her lower back—not pressing, not pushing—just there, quiet, anchoring her through the weight of every stare.

And then—Marcus.

Posted by his car, leaning against the hood, chain glinting, arms crossed, that same slick grin stretched wide. But the burn in his eyes? Not masked at all. A storm brewing, loud under the quiet.

The old heads by the grill noticed too, their conversation stalling, heads tilting slow as they tracked Jay, tracked Marcus, tracked the space between them.

The women by the dessert table whispered sharp, earrings swinging, cups of soda in hand, brows lifted, tongues quick behind lips glossed in beauty supply shine.

Her?

That fast?

Whole block gonna' blow…

The smell of charcoal, grease, cheap beer, and old history curled heavy through the air—thicker than smoke, louder than music.

And Jay? Still steady. Still posted. Eyes sliding to Marcus. Saying nothing—but saying everything.

Nia's chest tightened, but her feet kept moving. The block party might play like peace. But this? This was tension wrapped in plastic chairs and barbecue smoke. And it was one word away from blowing.

"I been calling'," he added, his voice dipping softer now — fake-sincere — but the undercurrent was sharp, irritated, unraveling.

Nia's jaw clenched, her pride raw under the hoodie, her stomach twisting tighter as Marcus closed the distance.

"You got folks looking' at me sideways," he muttered, voice low, layered with blame, his eyes burning into hers. "You really letting' the block spin this whole thing like I'm the problem?"

Jay's shoulder brushed faint against hers — steady, grounding — but his presence stayed unmoved, unbothered, posted like stone.

Nia's mouth opened, then closed. The words caught sharp in her throat, tangled in pride, nerves, history.

Marcus tilted his head, his grin curving sharp at the corners.

"Ain't like you got a lot of options now," he added, voice slick, dangerous at the edges. "I still got a say."

The words dropped heavy — louder than the block's whispers, sharper than the heat pressing down. The tension was thick enough to snap. And it wasn't done yet.

The hum of the fridge filled the kitchen — low, steady — the only sound holding space between all the words nobody had spoken yet. Nia's shoes sat by the door. Jay leaned against the frame. Brenda's hand lingered on the counter, fingers tapping slow, steady, sharp with quiet tension.

The cousins were posted at the table — Kia with her arms folded, one acrylic nail tapping against the wood; Keisha nursing a half-empty cup of coffee, eyes locked sharp on Nia like she already knew the whole story.

The weight in the room curled heavy under Nia's skin — thick as the Florida humidity clinging to the windows, sharp as the pride fighting to keep her upright. Brenda's eyes drifted to Jay — slow, unreadable — taking in his frame, the quiet set of his jaw, the hoodie clinging to Nia's shoulders.

The silence dragged long enough to stretch tight across Nia's chest. Then Kia broke it — her voice light, but edged with cousin-energy sharp enough to draw blood. "Whole block buzzing'," she muttered, her gaze flicking between them. "You know Marcus posted up talking' reckless, right?"

Keisha snorted — low, amused — her eyes sliding back to Nia.

"Seen it coming'," she added, her mouth curling faint. "You can only play tug-of-war so long before somebody get dragged."

Brenda's exhale was sharp — quiet, but final — her eyes cutting back to Nia, disappointment heavy without saying a word.

"You got more than just your pride on the line now," she said, her voice low, steady, the weight of years layered in every word. "Time to stop acting' like this ain't real."

The words landed hard — low in Nia's chest, pressing sharp behind her ribs, her pride bruising under the weight. Her fingers curled tight at her sides, hoodie sleeves bunching in her fists, her throat dry with everything she wanted to say but couldn't find the breath for.

Jay's presence stayed steady by the doorway — not interrupting, not flinching — just there. Quiet. Loud in his stillness. Loud in the way his eyes tracked Nia like he was reading every crack in her armor.

The room buzzed faint — fridge humming, clock ticking, cousins whispering low. But the weight? It pressed in heavy. And the words? They weren't done yet.

The hum of the old AC filled the apartment — steady, low, blending with the faint buzz of traffic creeping in through the half-cracked window. The fight's echo still lingered — sharp words hanging in the air like smoke that hadn't cleared yet.

Nia stood by the counter — fingers curled tight around the edge, her chest rising and falling uneven, the weight of what they'd just said pressing sharp behind her ribs. The kitchen light flickered faint, catching on the edges of the chipped counter top, the faded tiles cool under her bare feet.

Jay stayed still across the small space — his frame relaxed, but his eyes locked on her. Steady. Seeing every crack, every raw edge, reading her the way only he did.

The silence dragged — long, heavy — her pulse loud behind her ears, her throat tight with everything tangled in her chest. Jay's shoulders eased faint, his body shifting slow, careful, like he was giving her space to breathe, to settle, but still staying close enough to hold her steady if she folded.

Nia's eyes flicked up — cautious, raw — meeting his, the apartment shrinking down to the space between them.

Jay's voice broke the quiet — low, stripped down, heavy with honesty.

"I ain't mad," he said — not sharp, not tired — just steady. "You scared.

You carrying' too much.

I get that."

Nia's chest tightened, her grip on the counter loosening as the pride in her chest cracked quieter, her shoulders sagging faint. Her throat worked — dry, raw — the words crawling up behind her teeth.

"I'm… tired," she admitted, her voice small, rough, layered with the kind of exhaustion that sat heavy on the bones. "Tired of fighting'. Tired of… feeling' like I gotta hold it all."

Jay's brow furrowed faint, his eyes softening, the quiet understanding in his stare settling low in her chest.

"You ain't gotta hold it by yourself," he murmured, his steps slow, steady, closing the space between them inch by inch. "You been trying' to hold the whole world on your back. But you got me."

The words curled around her — real, steady — heavier than pride, louder than fear.

Her body softened as he stepped closer — the familiar warmth of him pressing into her space, the quiet buzz of the apartment fading behind the sound of her own uneven breath. Jay's hand lifted — slow, careful — brushing light along her jaw, his thumb tracing soft at the corner of her mouth.

"You good at building' walls," he added — not sharp, not teasing — just real. "But I been steady breaking' 'em down."

Nia's laugh broke — raw, tangled with nerves — her eyes stinging faint as the weight of his words settled low in her belly. The pride cracked. The fear loosened. And all that was left was him. Her. This moment.

Jay's forehead pressed light to hers — his arms curling gentle around her waist, pulling her slow against his chest, his heartbeat steady under her palms. Nia's eyes slipped closed, her body easing into him — the warmth of his hoodie, the solid rhythm of his breathing, the safety of his arms settling over the cracks in her pride like patchwork.

The apartment stayed quiet — the block still loud outside, the mess still waiting' — but for now, it was just them. Tangled. Raw. Real.

The rubble of the fight lay around them. But love? It was finally settling' in the cracks.

CHAPTER 11

"Everything on Front Street"

The block party buzzed low — bass still   thumping, grill smoke rolling, kids laughing distant — but under it, the energy shifted. Sharp. Heavy. Close to cracking.

Nia felt it first — the crawl of eyes tracking her and Jay as they crossed the lot, the quiet   hush rolling over   conversations like a wave.   Jay walked steady beside her, frame relaxed, hoodie sleeves pushed to his elbows — but his stare stayed locked, sharp, clocking every shift in the air.

Marcus leaned against   his car, arms crossed tight   over his chest, chain glinting sharp in the low sunlight.   His eyes burned, lingering on Nia, then cutting to Jay. And the block? It felt the storm brewing. Old heads paused their dominoes. Ladies by the food table slowed their conversations. Even the teens by the court stopped bouncing the ball.

Marcus pushed off the car slow — his steps casual, but the tension loud as hell, crawling up every wall   of the lot. Nia's chest tightened, her pride twisting raw, her stomach knotting as Marcus closed the space between them. His voice cut through the noise, loud enough for everybody to catch.

"Whole block watching, Ni," Marcus started, mouth twisted in a sharp grin that didn't touch his eyes. "Guess you ain't shy now, huh?"

Jay didn't flinch. Didn't speak. But the quiet undercurrent   in him shifted — steady but ready. Nia held her ground, chin lifted, nerves tangled tight under her skin, her voice coming low, sharp. "Why you always got to show out?" she bit, her words brittle with pride.

Marcus chuckled — dry, brittle — his eyes sliding over Jay like he wasn't even there.

"Show out? C'mon, Ni," Marcus tossed back, louder now, for the block, for the audience. "You the one showing out   — whole damn lot   talking 'bout how quick you switched teams.

"The words dropped heavy. A sharp hum rolled through the crowd — quiet laughs, low murmurs, the block leaning in.   Jay's hand slid to Nia's lower back — steady, anchoring — his eyes never   leaving Marcus, his stance still, his presence loud as ever.

"Let it go," Nia warned, her pride cracking, nerves pressing hard behind her ribs.

But Marcus was already too far gone. His grin widened, his voice slick.

"I ain't letting what's mine go that easy."

The lot got quiet. Music still playing, but muffled under the weight of eyes, of tension, of history crawling thick through the air.   Jay finally spoke — voice low, even, dangerous.

"She made a choice," he said, his stare locked, sharp. "Respect it."

The line drawn — sharp,   clear. The moment? One wrong word from exploding.

Marcus' jaw flexed, his pride bruising under his skin,   his ego spilling loud. And the block? Soaking it up, waiting for the crack.

The hum of the speakers barely filled the air anymore — old-school   soul tracks whispering low under   the suffocating silence stretching across the lot. The smell of smoke, cheap beer, and grilled meat sat heavy,   but none of it covered the tension burning up the street.

Marcus stood close now — frame tight, arms flexed across his chest, eyes locked on Jay with enough heat to boil pavement. The block stayed still as statues. Old heads leaning on car   hoods. Women posted by the food tables. Teens wide-eyed near the basketball court. All of them caught in the same sharp hush.

Nia's breath rattled low in her chest,   her pulse skipping, nerves crawling hot under her hoodie sleeves. Jay's hand stayed light at her lower back — not pressing, not claiming — just steady, quiet, loud in the stillness. Marcus' mouth curled sharp, but his eyes told on him — tired, hurt, pride spilling out, too bruised to hold back now.

"You real bold," Marcus tossed at Jay, voice low but slicing, meant for him but loud enough for the block to catch. "Walking 'round holding what I built." The words hung heavy. Nia's stomach twisted. The whispers bubbled quiet around them.

"That him?"

"Baby daddy mad mad…"

"Boy gone' fold in front the whole block…"

Jay's stare didn't move — eyes cool,   mouth tight, the kind of stillness that ain't weakness, it's patience ready to snap.

"Marcus, stop this," Nia's voice cracked out, sharp at the edges.But Marcus was already drowning in his pride. His grin widened — brittle, messy — his voice climbing sharper, ego spilling all over the cracked pavement.

"You forget where you from, Nia?" he fired back, eyes swinging to her, his words loud, bitter. "Whole lot of y'all switch up soon as some fake-solid dude stand next to you."

The crowd flinched — quiet   gasps, sharp exhales,   whispers riding the smoke rolling through the lot.   Jay stayed steady.   His hand eased up, sliding from her back to her wrist, his thumb pressing faint,   anchoring her. His voice came low, final.

"Say what you want 'bout me," Jay warned,   calm but layered with heat. "But you talk sideways to her again, it won't be words flying."

The block froze. Nothing but bass humming, chicken popping on the grill, hearts beating loud under skin.   Marcus' nostrils flared, his jaw flexed, his pride spilling out fast, wild, too messy to tuck back now.

"You think you built for this?" Marcus snapped, leaning in, his voice low but sharp. "It ain't just cookouts and whispers. You gonna' see."

Jay didn't blink. Didn't move. Just let the words float   dead in the air   — steady, cold, ready.

Nia's throat tightened. Her chest burned. The block feasted on every damn second of it. And her? She was standing dead center   — heart twisting, pride bruising, panic building.

And it still wasn't done.

The air stayed heavy — thick as the Florida humidity rolling low off   the pavement — every breath sticky, sharp, laced with tension that wouldn't let go. Marcus stepped back,   slow, measured, but the fire in his eyes still burned, the pride in him still   twisted, cracked, bleeding all   over his expression.

His arms crossed tight, chin lifted just enough to fake confidence, but his jaw locked, twitching, telling on him. Jay didn't move. Didn't blink. His hand stayed light at Nia's wrist, the warmth of his fingers the only thing steady in all the mess.

The crowd froze for half a second longer — like the lot itself had paused, waiting to see if fists fly, if words spill, if it really snapped wide open.

Nia's chest rose, her pulse heavy behind her ribs, her pride sitting sharp under her skin. Her eyes cut to the faces posted all around — every stare landing heavy, every whisper hanging low.

Kia stood by the dessert table, arms folded, mouth curled faint, eyes locked sharp on Nia like, See? You in it now. Keisha sipped her drink slow, side-eye heavy, lips pressed tight, reading every ounce of tension in the space.

The old heads leaned against cars, their faces stone quiet, but their eyes sharp, clocking it all. The women with their kids huddled near the picnic tables, mouths quiet but eyes flipping between Jay and Marcus,   their hands holding babies close like the street taught 'them what comes next. Even the teenagers perched on the basketball fence, wild-eyed, eating up every second like it was a movie playing live.

Marcus shifted — jaw flexing,   shoulders squaring like he might   run his mouth again — but his pride was already bruised,   already read by the block. And Jay? Still posted, still steady, still unreadable as stone.

The tension eased back — not   gone, just tucked under the buzz of whispers that picked up sharp now.

"Jay ain't blink…"

"Marcus tight…"

"Nia really picking' sides…"

"That whole block split now…"

Nia's pulse skipped — the weight of every stare, every word, every history-soaked moment dragging down on her chest. Jay's thumb brushed slow at her wrist — a quiet reminder, a steady choice. The lines drawn. The block ain't neutral no more. And neither was she.

The lot stretched wide and empty now — plastic chairs creaking faint in the breeze, foil on the food tables flapping soft, the smell of grease and smoke still curling in the air.   But all Nia could feel was the weight   — the raw, twisting mess of pride and fear crawling under her skin.

And Jay. Standing right there — steady, quiet, waiting. His hand hovered near her wrist still — not holding, not pressing — but   close enough she could still feel the warmth of him humming under her skin.

Nia's chest rose uneven, breath catching, pride clogging her   throat, her heart pounding too fast for words to find their way out. The block might've drifted off, music playing faint again, but the eyes? Still   out there. Still watching windows. Still whispering from porches.

Jay's voice broke the heavy quiet — low, calm, soft in a way that scraped at the nerves coiled tight in her chest.

"I ain't mad if you scared," he said, eyes locked on hers, steady, unreadable but honest. "I'd be more worried if you wasn't."

Nia blinked, her pride pulling sharp behind her eyes, but the fear softened, creeping quiet beneath the hard edges of her nerves. Her hands curled at her sides, hoodie sleeves twisting under her fingers.

"You make it sound easy," she shot back, her voice rough, eyes burning. "Like standing next to you don't come with a target."

Jay's jaw flexed faint, but his stare never wavered.

"I know it don't," he answered, low, even. "But I'm still here.

"The words landed heavy, sharp, louder than the block, louder than the whispers, louder than the fear crawling up her spine. Still here. Still posted. Still steady.

Nia's pride cracked faint — the tight grip of her fear unraveling just enough to breathe. She looked at him — really looked — at the quiet tension in his shoulders, the raw honesty sitting behind his eyes, the steady weight of him beside her like a shield she hadn't asked for but needed more than she wanted to admit.

The choice sat thick in the air. All in. Or not.

The block gonna' talk. Family gonna' press. Marcus? Ain't done. But this —
this moment — it was hers. Theirs.

Her voice caught low in her throat, not ready to say it yet. But her feet? Still
planted. Close to him. Facing the same direction. Already speaking for her.

Jay's eyes softened faint — no pressure, no smugness — just quiet
understanding.

"We got time," he added, voice low, steady. "But I need to know when you
ready — it's us. Or it ain't."

The hum of the block filled the quiet again — music rolling soft, laughter
drifting distant, the heat still pressing down.

But for Nia, the only thing real was him. And this moment. And the fear.
And the want. Tangled up together. But still steady. Still here.

CHAPTER 12

"Pressure Don't Let Up"

The screen door clicked soft behind them, the cool hum of the AC whispering faint over the buzz of the block still ringing in Nia's ears. The living room sat quiet — but not peaceful. Still. Tight. Air pressed thick against her chest. Brenda stood by the small kitchen counter, arms crossed, brows tight, mouth pursed in that way that said I already know, now you gonna' tell me anyway.

Jay eased in behind Nia, broad frame filling the doorway, presence quiet but steady, his eyes reading the room like he'd walked into a war zone before. Nia's heart tapped quick behind her ribs, her hoodie clinging faint to her back, pride raw under her skin. The couch still held the indent from where Brenda had been sitting earlier, the remote on the cushion, the TV muted, but the weight of old conversations floated heavy in the air.

Brenda's stare slid from Nia to Jay, lingered there a second longer, then cut back to her daughter. "You good?" Brenda asked, voice low, tight — but the question wasn't about health. It was about sense. About choices. About the mess on the block they had just walked through.

Nia's throat worked, her hands curling faint at her sides.

"I'm good," she answered, quiet, layered with pride, nerves crawling under her skin.

Brenda's brow arched. Her arms stayed crossed. The silence stretched long enough to burn. "You wanna explain," she pressed, voice still low, sharp edges tucked just under it, "how you out there with everybody and they mama watching, Marcus running his mouth, and you—" her eyes flicked to Jay, "—standing right beside him?"

The words hit soft, but heavy. Jay stayed posted — hands loose in his pockets, expression steady — letting Nia speak, letting the room unfold slow. Nia's pulse quickened, pride bruising, mouth dry.

"We not... we—" her voice cracked faint, nerves twisting, but the heat in her chest forced it out. "We together."

Brenda's stare held steady. No flinch. No sigh. Just eyes sharp enough to peel pride back layer by layer. "You sure?" she asked — soft, real, not cruel — but laced with the weight of a mother's fear.

Nia exhaled slow — pride fraying, nerves unraveling — but her feet stayed planted. Her words still came. "Yeah," she said, voice stronger now, eyes locking on her mama's. "I'm sure."

The room stayed quiet. The block buzzed low outside. Jay stayed posted, quiet, steady. Brenda's shoulders eased faint, her arms uncrossing, but her expression was still guarded, still layered, still watching.

"We gonna' talk," she said, voice low but final. "But tonight? Eat something'. Sit down. Y'all both look like you ran through hell."

Nia's chest loosened faint — not gone, not easy — but lighter. Jay finally moved, stepping in slow, steady, his hand sliding light to her lower back, quiet support, no pressure. The house wasn't peaceful. But it was holding. For now.

The hum of the AC filled the small apartment — faint, steady — but underneath it, the street noise crept in. Sharp. Clear. Loud in ways it wasn't supposed to be. Nia stood by the window, hoodie sleeves twisting under her fingers, her eyes slipping to the cracked glass, her chest tight with nerves crawling under her skin.

Jay sat on the edge of the couch, hoodie pushed to his elbows, broad frame leaned forward, elbows on his knees. Still, but his eyes were sharp, reading every sound floating through the walls. Outside, the block buzzed low — conversations riding the air, sneakers scuffing concrete, the occasional bark of laughter that didn't sound real. But layered under that was the tension. The whispers. The weight of Marcus' pride floating heavy through the neighborhood.

The phone on the counter buzzed. Kia's name lit the screen. Nia snatched it quick, thumb sliding across, her cousin's voice spilling fast, coated in nerves and irritation. "You hearing' this?" Kia snapped, sharp over the line. "He out. Loud."

Nia's throat tightened, stomach twisting, pride prickling. "Where?" she shot back, eyes flicking toward Jay.

"Everywhere," Kia answered, frustration spilling fast. "Corner store, liquor spot, chilling' by them benches — running' his mouth like you all ain't just shut him down at the lot."

Jay's eyes locked on hers, steady, unshaken, but his shoulders squared faint, the calm in him edged now. Kia kept going. "He talking' crazy, Ni," she said, voice low but sharp. "Saying' you confused, saying' he letting' you get your space but you gonna' 'circle back.'"

The words hit sour, heavy — the familiar sting of Marcus twisting stories to save his pride. Jay's jaw flexed faint, quiet   patience fraying. "He dragging' Jay too,"   Kia added,   bitterness lacing her   words. "Not by name,   but everybody know. Saying' 'dudes like that' don't last, saying' 'real ones stay, fake ones flex.' You know how he do."

Nia's stomach coiled tighter,   pride twisting,   nerves crawling hot under her skin. Jay stood, slow, steady, stepping toward her. His hand slid faint to her waist, thumb pressing light against the curve of her side, anchoring her.

The buzz of the block seeped through the window — louder now. Laughter. Sneaker scuffs. And faint, sharp words they weren't meant to hear.

"…he really just letting' it happen?"

"…heard Marcus at the store saying' he ain't worried…"

"…girl picking' the wrong one…"

Nia's pulse jumped, pride raw, heart twisting tight behind her ribs.

"We shut that down?" Kia asked, voice low, cousin-protective, ready for mess.

Nia's breath rattled faint.   Her eyes on Jay.   His hand steady.   His stare steady. His calm, loud as ever. "No," she answered,   her voice rough but sure. "Let him talk."

Kia sighed sharp, tight.

"Talking' ain't all he do," she warned. "Just… keep your head up."

The call clicked off. The buzz of the block rolled back in.   Jay's thumb brushed faint against her side. Steady. Quiet. But layered with promise.

"He can talk,"   Jay murmured,   voice low,   steady, dangerous under the softness. "But we still here."

The street noise hummed. The tension crawled. The whispers stuck to the window like condensation. Marcus wasn't done. But neither were they.

The door clicked soft behind them, the familiar creak of the screen door stretching open, the sharp slap as it swung shut again. But the air outside? It wasn't familiar anymore. It was different. Thicker. Heavy with eyes.

The pavement stayed warm under   Nia's sneakers, even with the sun dipped low, the humid buzz of Florida clinging to her skin like sweat   that wouldn't quit. Jay walked steady beside her, broad frame relaxed, shoulders loose, but his eyes were sharp,   moving, clocking every glance, every shift in energy as they stepped down.

The block buzzed low — quiet   conversations curled under the hum of a box fan spinning in somebody's window,   the faint clatter of domino's on a porch, the sharp sizzle of a cigarette cherry flaring in the dusk. But under it was tension. Whispers. Weight.

Mrs. Carter sat on her porch, hand-fan working slow,   eyes sliding over them behind oversize sunglasses that didn't hide a thing. Her mouth didn't move, but her stare spoke clear. Two old heads leaned against the fence, arms crossed, heads tilted faint, their conversation pausing as Nia and Jay passed, the sharp hum of their quiet words floating behind them.

"That's him…"

"Marcus tight, you know he ain't done…"

"She really out here choosing'…"

Nia's chest tightened, pride prickling, nerves crawling, but her chin stayed lifted, her steps steady. Jay's hand brushed faint at the small of her back — not claiming, not pressing — just   steady. Quiet anchor. Loud without saying a word.

The teenagers   by the court   slowed their   dribble, ball bouncing soft, sneakers scuffing, eyes tracking as they crossed the lot.   Even the dogs barked quieter now. Even the block was breathing different.   The whispers followed — soft, sharp, heavy.

"Marcus saying' he letting' her 'cool off'…"

"Jay too quiet, that's the one you watch…"

"She bold walking' out here like that…"

The air pressed tight. The glances sharper. The whole block leaning in. But Nia's steps stayed steady. And Jay's presence stayed loud as ever.   They weren't hiding. They weren't folding. Not tonight.

The sun sank low behind the rooftops, the sky stretching soft with blue and deep orange, the faint hum of streetlights buzzing to life across the lot. The block settled quiet. Porches emptied.

Conversations tucked behind screen doors. Even the dogs gone quiet. But the weight lingered — heavy, like the thick summer heat   that wouldn't lift off the pavement.

Nia leaned back against the stoop, arms folded, hoodie sleeves bunched at her elbows, chest tight, nerves crawling, pride raw but   settled. Jay sat beside her, legs stretched out,   arms loose over   his knees, broad frame relaxed, eyes soft. Watching her. Steady.

The streetlamps clicked faint, glow spilling soft over the sidewalk, shadows stretching long under   their feet. For once, the whispers were gone.   The block wasn't watching. Wasn't listening. Just quiet. Just them.

Nia exhaled slow, breath shaky, the tension still twisting low in her chest, but the fear was easing now,   softening under   the steady hum of   Jay's presence. "You good?" he asked,   voice low, rough from the long day,   but honest. Real.

Nia's lips pressed tight, pride fighting to hold the words back, but her body was already leaning toward him.   Already done pretending she didn't   feel safer near him than anywhere else. She nodded faint, her voice small, but the choice already made.

"I'm good," she said, quiet, real. "I'm just… tired."

Jay's mouth curved faint — not   a full smile, but something soft, understanding, layered with the same exhaustion she felt under her ribs. "We still here," he murmured, voice low, final. Like it was enough. Like they didn't need speeches. Didn't need promises yet. Just presence.

Nia's shoulders eased, pride loosening, nerves quieting. The block was still heavy. Marcus still lurking. Family still talking. But them? Still here. Still standing. Still side by side.

And tonight, that was enough.

CHAPTER 13

"It Ain't Over"

The heat still rolled low off the pavement. Even with the sun setting, the air clung heavy to Jay's skin as he crossed the lot. Nia stayed by the porch — posted, arms folded, eyes scanning the street — but Jay already caught the look.

Old Mr. Curtis leaned against the corner store wall, cigarette burning slow between his fingers, eyes sharp beneath the brim of his faded Marlins cap. He didn't wave him over, didn't call out. Just nodded. Subtle. Loud enough if you knew how to listen.

Jay eased over — steps steady, shoulders loose — but his chest already tight with the weight of what he knew was coming.

Mr. Curtis dragged on his cigarette, smoke curling out the side of his mouth, eyes never leaving the street. "You solid?" he asked — voice low, lined with years of block history.

Jay nodded faintly, leaning his shoulder to the wall, his eyes sweeping the lot. "I'm good."

Mr. Curtis chuckled low — not amused, just layered with quiet knowledge. "Good don't last long round here when pride's bruised," he muttered, eyes cutting toward Jay. "And that boy Marcus? He bleeding all over the place."

Jay's jaw flexed faintly, but his stance stayed steady. "He talking'," Jay said.

Mr. Curtis shook his head, slow, certain. "Nah," he corrected, voice sharper now. "He moving'. You ain't new — you know what that mean."

"I'm good," she answered, quiet, layered with pride, nerves crawling under her skin.

Brenda's brow arched. Her arms stayed crossed. The silence stretched long enough to burn. "You wanna explain," she pressed, voice still low, sharp edges tucked just under it, "how you out there with everybody and they mama watching, Marcus running his mouth, and you—" her eyes flicked to Jay, "—standing right beside him?"

The words hit soft, but heavy. Jay stayed posted — hands loose in his pockets, expression steady — letting Nia speak, letting the room unfold slow. Nia's pulse quickened, pride bruising, mouth dry. "We not... we—" her voice cracked faint, nerves twisting, but the heat in her chest forced it out. "We together."

Brenda's stare held steady. No flinch. No sigh. Just eyes sharp enough to peel pride back layer   by layer. "You sure?" she asked — soft,   real, not cruel — but laced with the weight of a mother's fear.

Nia exhaled slow — pride fraying, nerves unraveling — but her feet stayed planted. Her words still came. "Yeah," she said, voice stronger now, eyes locking on her mama's. "I'm sure."

The room stayed quiet. The block buzzed low outside. Jay stayed posted, quiet, steady. Brenda's shoulders eased faint, her arms uncrossing, but her expression was still guarded, still layered, still watching.

"We gonna' talk," she said, voice low but final. "But tonight? Eat something'. Sit down. Y'all both look like you ran through hell."

Nia's chest loosened faint — not gone, not easy — but lighter. Jay finally moved, stepping in slow, steady, his hand sliding light to her lower back, quiet support, no pressure. The house wasn't peaceful. But it was holding. For now.

The hum of   the AC filled the small   apartment — faint, steady — but underneath it, the street noise crept in. Sharp. Clear. Loud in ways it wasn't supposed to be. Nia stood by the window,   hoodie sleeves twisting under her fingers, her eyes slipping to the cracked glass, her chest tight
with nerves crawling under her skin.

Jay sat on the edge of   the couch, hoodie pushed to his elbows,   broad frame leaned forward, elbows on his knees. Still, but his eyes were sharp, reading every sound floating through the walls.   Outside, the block buzzed low — conversations riding the air, sneakers scuffing concrete,
the occasional bark of laughter that didn't sound real. But layered under that was the tension. The whispers. The weight of Marcus' pride floating heavy through the neighborhood.

The phone on the counter buzzed. Kia's name lit the screen. Nia snatched it quick, thumb sliding across,   her cousin's voice spilling fast,   coated in nerves and irritation. "You hearing' this?" Kia snapped, sharp over the line. "He out. Loud."

Nia's throat tightened, stomach twisting, pride prickling.

"Where?" she shot back, eyes flicking toward Jay.

"Everywhere," Kia answered, frustration spilling fast. "Corner store, liquor spot, chilling' by them benches — running' his mouth like you all ain't just shut him down at the lot."

Jay's eyes locked on hers, steady, unshaken, but his shoulders squared faint, the calm in him edged now. Kia kept going. "He talking' crazy, Ni," she said, voice low but sharp. "Saying' you confused, saying' he letting' you get your space but you gonna' 'circle back.'"

The words hit sour, heavy — the familiar sting of Marcus twisting stories to save his pride. Jay's jaw flexed faint, quiet patience fraying. "He dragging' Jay too," Kia added, bitterness lacing her words. "Not by name, but everybody know. Saying' 'dudes like that' don't last, saying' 'real ones stay, fake ones flex.' You know how he do."

Nia's stomach coiled tighter, pride twisting, nerves crawling hot under her skin. Jay stood, slow, steady, stepping toward her. His hand slid faint to her waist, thumb pressing light against the curve of her side, anchoring her. The buzz of the block seeped through the window — louder now. Laughter. Sneaker scuffs. And faint, sharp words they weren't meant to hear.

"…he really just letting' it happen?"

"…heard Marcus at the store saying' he ain't worried…"

"…girl picking' the wrong one…"

Nia's pulse jumped, pride raw, heart twisting tight behind her ribs. "We shut that down?" Kia asked, voice low, cousin-protective, ready for mess.

Nia's breath rattled faint. Her eyes on Jay. His hand steady. His stare steady. His calm, loud as ever. "No," she answered, her voice rough but sure. "Let him talk."

Kia sighed sharp, tight. "Talking' ain't all he do," she warned. "Just… keep your head up."

The call clicked off. The buzz of the block rolled back in. Jay's thumb brushed faint against her side. Steady. Quiet. But layered with promise. "He can talk," Jay murmured, voice low, steady, dangerous under the softness. "But we still here."

The street noise hummed. The tension crawled. The whispers stuck to the window like condensation. Marcus wasn't done. But neither were they.

The door clicked soft behind them, the familiar creak of the screen door stretching open, the sharp slap as it swung shut again. But the air outside? It wasn't familiar anymore. It was different. Thicker. Heavy with eyes.

The pavement stayed warm under Nia's sneakers, even with the sun dipped low, the humid buzz of Florida clinging to her skin like sweat that wouldn't quit. Jay walked steady beside her, broad frame relaxed, shoulders loose, but his eyes were sharp, moving, clocking every glance, every shift in energy as they stepped down.

The block buzzed low — quiet conversations curled under the hum of a box fan spinning in somebody's window, the faint clatter of domino's on a porch, the sharp sizzle of a cigarette cherry flaring in the dusk. But under it was tension. Whispers. Weight.

Mrs. Carter sat on her porch, hand-fan working slow, eyes sliding over them behind oversize sunglasses that didn't hide a thing. Her mouth didn't move, but her stare spoke clear. Two old heads leaned against the fence, arms crossed, heads tilted faint, their conversation pausing as Nia and Jay passed, the sharp hum of their quiet words floating behind them.

"That's him…"

"Marcus tight, you know he ain't done…"

"She really out here choosing'…"

Nia's chest tightened, pride prickling, nerves crawling, but her chin stayed lifted, her steps steady. Jay's hand brushed faint at the small of her back — not claiming, not pressing — just steady. Quiet anchor. Loud without saying a word.

The teenagers by the court slowed their dribble, ball bouncing soft, sneakers scuffing, eyes tracking as they crossed the lot. Even the dogs barked quieter now. Even the block was breathing different. The whispers followed — soft, sharp, heavy.

"Marcus saying' he letting' her 'cool off'…"

"Jay too quiet, that's the one you watch…"

"She bold walking' out here like that…"

The air pressed tight. The glances sharper. The whole block leaning in. But Nia's steps stayed steady. And Jay's presence stayed loud as ever.   They weren't hiding. They weren't folding. Not tonight.

The sun sank low behind the rooftops, the sky stretching soft with blue and deep orange, the faint hum of streetlights buzzing to life across the lot. The block settled quiet. Porches emptied. Conversations tucked behind screen doors. Even the dogs gone quiet. But the weight lingered — heavy, like the thick summer heat that wouldn't lift off the pavement.

Nia leaned back against the stoop, arms folded, hoodie sleeves bunched at her elbows, chest tight, nerves crawling, pride raw but settled. Jay sat beside her, legs stretched out, arms loose over his knees, broad frame relaxed, eyes soft. Watching her. Steady.

The streetlamps clicked faint, glow spilling soft over the sidewalk, shadows stretching long under their feet. For once, the whispers were gone.   The block wasn't watching. Wasn't listening. Just quiet. Just them.

Nia exhaled slow, breath shaky, the tension still twisting low in her chest, but the fear was easing now,   softening under the steady hum of   Jay's presence. "You good?" he asked, voice low, rough from the long day,   but honest. Real.

The street hummed low: car doors slamming, music drifting, a distant bark of a dog. But under it lingered that same tension, that same quiet storm brewing.

Jay exhaled slow, his shoulders squaring, eyes sharp. "I ain't looking' for that," he muttered, voice low but real.

"Don't matter what you looking' for," Curtis fired back,   cigarette burning down to the filter. "It looking' for you now."

The words landed low and heavy,   sticking to the humid air.   Jay's hand flexed at his side, pulse steady but his mind already clocking the moves. "Appreciate it," he said, nodding once, quiet.

Curtis tapped the ash from his cigarette, his eyes sliding to Nia standing by the porch — small but steady, pride wrapped tight around her shoulders like armor.

"You holding' her down," he added, voice low, final. "That make you a target — not just her."

Jay's eyes stayed locked on Nia. "I know," he answered. "But I'm still here."

The old man chuckled — sharp, real — flicked the cigarette to the ground, the last of the smoke curling away. "Then be ready," Curtis warned, pushing off the wall, steps slow down the block. "It ain't over."

Jay stayed posted a second longer, the street humming quiet, the warning heavy in his chest. It wasn't over. Not yet. But he was ready.

The front door clicked soft behind them — the faint hum of the old AC floating through the apartment, the buzz of the TV low in the background. But the quiet wasn't real. It was just the pause before the voices spilled over.

Kia leaned against the kitchen counter, arms crossed, eyes sharp, mouth already curled like she'd been waiting. Keisha perched on the arm of the couch, phone in hand, eyes lifting, brows arched, mouth tight. Brenda stood by the sink — dish towel hanging loose in her hand, stare locked on Nia, sharp, tired, laced with that mama-love that sound sweet but hit hard.

The air pressed in tight — the kind of quiet that ain't peaceful, just heavy with what ain't been said yet. Jay filled the doorway behind Nia — broad frame solid, eyes sweeping the room, quiet, steady, unshaken.

The TV flickered muted commercials across the small living room, but nobody was watching.

Kia spoke first — voice light, but sharp under it. "So, y'all famous now," she tossed, eyes sliding between them. "Whole block buzzing'."

Keisha snorted — low, bitter — her eyes cutting to Jay, mouth twisting. "Marcus out here acting' a fool," she added, "but it's you two they whispering' 'bout."

Brenda's exhale cut through the room, sharp, final. Her eyes stayed steady on Nia.

"You ready for this?" she asked, voice low, real, no sugar-coating.

Nia's throat worked — pride raw under her skin — but her feet stayed planted, her voice rising steady. "I'm ready," she answered, quiet but layered with heat.

Brenda's eyes narrowed faintly, sliding to Jay — slow, measured. "You?" she asked, same tone, same weight.

Jay's mouth pressed tight — no flinch, no fold. His answer came low, steady. "Been ready."

Kia laughed sharp. "Y'all cute," she muttered, rolling her eyes. "But you know how this block get. Pride ain't never just words. Marcus? He ain't done."

Keisha nodded, arms folding tight across her chest. "Everybody wanna be seen till the heat show up," she fired, eyes locking on Nia. "You sure you ready to stand in that?"

The air thickened, the apartment small, the weight of family pressing in. But Nia didn't fold. Not now. Her chin lifted, voice sharper. "I ain't running'," she shot back. "You can question me. The block can whisper. But I'm standing'."

Brenda's eyes softened faintly — pride, fear, exhaustion tangled behind them — but her mouth stayed firm. "Then stand," she said, voice low, final. "But don't forget — this block? It remember everything."

Jay's hand brushed light at Nia's back — steady, quiet support. The tension wasn't gone. The whispers hadn't stopped. But the house knew where she stood now. And who was standing with her.

CHAPTER 14

"The Block Pickin' Sides"

The hum of the old AC unit   filled the apartment — low, faint — but the air
still pressed hot, sticky against Nia's skin as she leaned into the edge of
the counter. The window cracked just enough to let the street in: the buzz
of voices drifting, faint music spilling from a porch speaker, the sharp bark
of a dog somewhere down the lot.

But under all that?

The tension.

Creeping.

Crawling.

Floating in quiet but real.

Jay stood a few steps off   — hoodie sleeves   shoved to his elbows,
shoulders loose, frame steady — but   his eyes kept moving, clocking the
energy through the walls,   same way she could feel   it crawl under her
hoodie.

Nia's phone buzzed sharp on the counter — screen lighting up with Kia's
name, bright, urgent. She snatched it up quick, thumb sliding fast, phone
pressed to her ear.

"Girl," Kia's voice snapped through the line — low, sharp, buzzing with the
block noise behind her — "you hear this mess yet?"

Nia's pulse jumped. Pride tight. Heart twisting. "What mess?" she asked,
voice tight, eyes cutting toward Jay.

His stare already locked on her — quiet,   steady — his brows lifted faint,
reading the nerves flashing across her face.

Kia laughed sharp — bitter   under the sound. "Block picking' sides," she
answered, voice fast, heavy. "You ain't even been out there five minutes
and they showing' colors."

Nia's stomach flipped,   nerves twisting raw under   her ribs. "Who?" she
asked, throat tight, pride bruising.

Kia snorted.

"Who ain't?" she fired back. "Old heads chill — saying' 'let her be grown.' But them porch mouth aunties? Messy as hell. Same ones that called you strong last week out here riding' for Marcus like he God's gift."

Nia's breath caught — pride, history, nerves all tangled. Jay moved in slow, steady, his hand sliding light to her waist, his thumb pressing faint against her side.

Kia's voice dropped lower — street caution layered under cousin-love. "He talking' calm," she added. "Real smooth, real collected. But he stirring'. You know how he do."

Nia exhaled slow — pride simmering, fear twisting, heart pounding too loud in her chest. Jay's hand stayed steady, warm, anchoring. "They loud wit' it?" Nia pressed, voice low, raw.

"Some," Kia sighed. "Some playing' neutral — but it's clear. You ain't invisible out there no more. Watch your step. And keep him close."

Nia's grip tightened on the phone,   nerves crawling hot under her hoodie sleeves. Jay leaned in — his voice low, for her alone.

"Let 'em talk," he muttered, eyes sharp, presence steady. "We still here." Her pride? Still cracked.

But her feet? Still planted.

Her body? Already leaning toward him.

The block was talking.

The sides were picked.

But them? Still standing.

The front door clicked soft behind them, evening air rolling in thick, humid, heavy on the skin.   The sidewalk   stretched wide under   their feet — pavement cracked, patches of grass peeking through,   faint glow of streetlights spilling dull across the block.

Nia's hoodie clung faint to her arms, her pulse knocking steady behind her ribs, nerves crawling up her spine. Jay walked steady beside her — broad frame posted solid, shoulders loose — but his eyes stayed sharp, moving, clocking every shadow, every sound.

The corner store sat a few lots down — neon OPEN sign buzzing low, door propped halfway with a brick. The block buzzed soft: porch chairs creaking, low conversations spilling, sharp clack of dominoes from a backyard table. But under all that? The tension. The split. The sides.

Nia caught the first glance before they even hit the corner — Ms. Carter posted on her steps, hand-fan working slow, eyes following them from behind her dollar-store sunglasses. Her mouth didn't move. But her stare said enough.

Further down, two women leaned against a porch railing — arms crossed, eyes cutting sharp, their conversation hushing' as Nia and Jay passed. The words low. But the energy? Loud.

"She still riding' with him…"

"Marcus gonna' act up for real soon…"

"She bold, I'll give her that…"

Jay's hand brushed faint at the small of Nia's back — not claiming, not pressing — just steady. Quiet anchor. Loud presence.

They crossed the lot, every step dragging more eyes. Old heads posted by the fence nodded faint, no words, but respect tucked quiet in the gesture. Teenagers perched on the curb paused — wide eyes, mouths curled with curiosity, sneakers tapping against the cracked pavement.

The split was clear now. Ain't no maybe. Some riding' for them. Some waiting' for them to fold.

They stepped into the corner store — cool air hitting sharp against the humidity outside. The cashier, Mr. Ellis, lifted his chin in greeting — eyes flicking quick over them, expression unreadable.

Two dudes by the back freezer posted up — low voices, sharp eyes, mouths tight. Jay clocked 'em — steady, shoulders squaring faint, his hand sliding to Nia's lower back as they moved through the aisle.

Nia's heart tapped quick, nerves prickling, pride simmering. The whispers weren't just whispers now. It was eyes. It was energy. It was split, clear as day.

The block had picked sides.

But them? Still moving.

Still steady.

Ain't no folding. Not tonight.

The apartment door clicked shut behind them — soft, but the air inside was heavy, tight, pressing. The hum of the AC buzzed low, but the sharp scent of fried food and leftover tension hit first.

Brenda posted by the kitchen sink — arms crossed,   eyes steady,   face unreadable but   loud without a word. Kia sat on the worn couch — leg bouncing, nails tapping on the armrest,   her stare sharp with cousin-curiosity and judgment   rolled together. Keisha leaned against the counter — arms folded,   phone in hand,   mouth already curled like she'd been waiting.

The TV played low — news running — but nobody listening.

Nia's pulse thudded behind her   ribs, hoodie sleeves twisting under   her fingers as she crossed the room.   Jay posted steady behind her — broad, quiet, eyes moving, presence thick.

Brenda's voice cut   first — low, layered, laced with that   tired, protective mama-tone that wasn't asking, just stating. "Whole block talkin'."

Kia smirked, tossing her head faint. "Not even five minutes out there," she added, "and it's already teams."

Keisha's eyes slid to Jay, mouth twisting sharp. "And y'all   still walkin' like you above it," she tossed. "Gotta respect the confidence."

Nia's jaw tightened — pride cracking,   nerves crawling — but   her feet stayed planted. "I ain't ask for nobody to pick teams," she fired back, voice low, rough. "But I ain't hidin' either."

Brenda's brow lifted faint, eyes locking sharp on hers. "You can't hide now," Brenda corrected, voice even. "The minute you step out with him — you chose your team."

Jay's hand brushed faint at Nia's back — steady,   quiet, the only soft thing in the room. Nia's chest squeezed, pride tight, heart heavy.

Kia's laugh cracked sharp, cutting through the room. "She riding'," she muttered. "Might as well own it."

Keisha's stare stayed hard on Jay — eyes sliding over him, mouth pressed tight. "Hope you built for it," she shot low. "This block? It'll eat you if you ain't."

Jay's mouth stayed firm, his voice coming low, real. "Been built for worse," he answered, eyes never leaving hers.

The air thickened — kitchen humming, family buzzing, tension hanging off the walls. Brenda exhaled slow — arms uncrossing, eyes heavy on Nia. "You sure?" she asked again — real, honest, not cruel — but layered with every ounce of worry only a mother can carry.

Nia swallowed hard. Her pride? Still bruised. But her choice? Loud. "I'm sure," she answered — voice rough, real, final.

The room didn't ease. The whispers didn't stop. But the choice? Planted. Loud. Hers.

The apartment settled quiet — the hum of the AC, the lower of the fridge, faint music spilling through the cracked window from down the block. The cousins' footsteps faded, front door clicking soft, the last sharp glances and quiet warnings drifting out with them.

Brenda's bedroom door shut low — the tired weight of her worry leaving the kitchen stretched empty.

Nia stood by the window — arms folded,   nerves crawling faint under her hoodie sleeves, eyes drifting to the block outside. The streetlights buzzed, porch shadows stretching long, sidewalk cracked and uneven, still carrying the echoes of earlier whispers.

Jay moved in slow — broad frame steady behind her,   his presence rolling quiet but warm across her back. He didn't speak yet. Didn't need to. His hand slid light   to her   waist, fingers pressing faint   against her side, anchoring her through the hum of nerves still twisting.

Nia exhaled slow — chest tight, heart heavy — but her feet stayed planted. Her body leaned back toward him, almost without thinking.

The apartment small, quiet. But the outside? Still loud. Still divided.

But them?

They were moving together. Solid.

Jay's voice cut   low, real soft, for her alone. "We gone' let 'em talk," he murmured, thumb drifting slow over her hoodie. "But they gonna' see
us standing'."

Nia's eyes slipped closed — her pride raw, her fear pressing, but his voice steady, the truth wrapped tight around it. Her hand slid back, fingers curling faint at his wrist, the unspoken hanging there between their skin.

They weren't folding.

They weren't drifting.

They were moving as one.The block? Can talk.

The family? Can question.

Marcus? Can lurk.

But them? Still standing. Still here.

Still moving together.

CHAPTER
15

"Love Ain't Safe, But It's Ours"

The apartment sat still, the quiet hum of the AC floating' faint through the vents, the fridge ticking' soft in the kitchen. Outside, the block buzzed low — porch chairs creaking', distant bass riding' the air from a parked car down the street, faint laughter drifting' somewhere past the corner. But inside, the silence pressed thick, heavy, unspoken words filling' every inch of space.

Nia sat curled on the edge of the worn couch, hoodie sleeves bunched at her elbows, hands twisted in the fabric, chest tight, mind crawling' with all the noise the block left behind. Jay leaned against the door frame — arms loose over his chest, broad shoulders relaxed — but his eyes were moving', steady, reading' the air the same way she could feel it crackling' soft around them. Her pulse tapped hard under her skin, pride bruised, nerves tight — but her feet were still planted. Still here.

The TV glowed low in the background, muted commercials spilling' soft light across the small living room — but nobody was watching'. Jay's gaze slid slow across the space — to the window cracked just enough for the street to creep in, to the scuffed floorboards, then finally back to her.

"You good?" he asked, voice low, rough, cutting' through the quiet.

Nia's breath caught — pride prickling', heart twisting' — but her mouth stayed dry, her chest still tight. The silence hung heavy. Not awkward. Just... full. Of fear. Of pride. Of mess. Of the feelings crawling' between them for weeks now. Jay's jaw flexed faint, but he didn't push. Didn't crowd. Just waited. Steady.

The air buzzed with the hum of the block outside — the distant echo of footsteps, a car door slamming', a shout drifting' from down the street. But in here, it was just them. Just the tension. Just the choice still hanging'. Nia swallowed hard, her voice rough, words fighting' through her chest.

"I'm good," she answered — quiet, layered, not sure she even believed it yet.

Jay's brow lifted faint, his stare locked steady. "You sure?" he pressed — not judging', not pushing', just real.

Nia's shoulders eased faint, pride unraveling', the fear crawling' low. "I don't know," she admitted, voice low, rough at the edges. "But I'm here.

"The words settled heavy. Clear. Jay's mouth curved faint — not a smile, just… understanding'. Quiet. Real. The silence stayed heavy, but softer now. Like maybe it didn't always have to be loud to be real.

The couch creaked faint beneath her as Nia shifted — knees tucked up, fingers twisting' in the fabric of her hoodie sleeves, heart pounding' low behind her ribs. Jay stayed posted by the door frame, broad frame leaning' slight, arms sliding' down to his sides now, eyes locked steady on her. The apartment buzzed quiet — AC humming', faint street noise drifting' through the cracked window — but the air was heavy. Full. Ready to snap open.

Nia's throat worked, pride fighting' the words, nerves crawling' up her spine — but her chest was too tight to keep it in.

"I ain't used to… this," she admitted,   eyes sliding' to the floor, pride raw, words rough at the edges.

Jay's brow lifted faint,   his eyes softening' under the steady. "This?" he echoed — quiet, patient, real.

Nia nodded, chin tucked, breath shaky. "Somebody standing' there," she added, voice rough, low, barely above a whisper. "When it get messy."

The hum of the AC rolled soft. The street outside buzzed faint. But in here? It was just them. Just the mess. Just the real.

Jay pushed off the door frame slow — steps quiet,   steady — closing' the space but not crowding'. His voice cut low through the quiet.

"I ain't ask you to be used to it," he said, voice rough, honest, warm in that way that scraped at the nerves. "But I'm still here."

Nia's chest twisted — fear   crawling', pride bruising' — but the words cracked open.

"I'm scared," she admitted, real, raw, breath shaking'. "Of losing' it. Of… wanting' it. Of this." Her hand lifted faint, gesturing' between them.

Jay's eyes stayed locked — unflinching',   steady. "I ain't," he said — voice low, final. "Scared or not — we here."

The words landed heavy. Real. Louder than the mess outside. Nia's mouth trembled faint — pride loosening, nerves unraveling'. Her eyes slid to his — meeting' steady, warm, honest. The fear was still there. But the walls? Starting' to crack. The words? Spilling' now. Finally.

The air in the apartment hung warm — the hum of the AC rolling' faint, the steady click of the fridge in the corner, soft shadows stretching' across the floorboards. Nia sat still, knees pulled up, hoodie sleeves bunched around her wrists, her hands curled faint at her sides. But her chest was loosening now, pride fraying', fear unraveling'.

Jay stood close — broad frame relaxed,   shoulders eased down,   his presence quiet but filling' the whole room.   The air between them was thin now, warm, charged with the weight of what they hadn't been saying'.

Her eyes drifted slow, sliding' up to his. The tension eased, but the nerves were still crawling' soft under her skin. Jay's hand moved — careful,   slow — sliding' down to brush faint at the fabric of her sleeve, his thumb grazing' the soft inside of her wrist. The heat of it settled under her skin — quiet but loud enough to make her heart stutter.

Her fingers lifted — hesitant, real — slid against his wrist, her grip feather-light but holding' him there. For a second, they just stayed. Breath mingling', the quiet buzz of the street drifting' faint through the cracked window. No rush. No fronting'. Just the small space closing' soft between them.

Jay leaned in — not fast, not pressing' — just moving' toward her like he had all the time in the world to let   her decide. His forehead lowered, brushed gentle to hers,   his eyes sliding' shut, breath warm against   her cheek.

Nia's pulse jumped, nerves twisting', but her body was already leaning'   in. Already letting' go.

The fear wasn't gone. The pride wasn't   fixed. The block was still   loud outside. But here, in this room, in this quiet, it felt… real. Safe in the only way it could be — messy, raw, theirs.

Jay's voice cracked low — quiet,   rough, breath brushing' against her lips. "You ain't gotta be perfect," he murmured. "You just gotta be here."

Nia's chest   squeezed, heart pounding' soft, her eyes slid closed,   her forehead staying' pressed to his.

"I'm here," she whispered, voice rough, honest. "I'm here."

The space between them was gone now.   The mess still   outside. But the love? Settling' in. Slow. Real. Theirs.

The hum of the AC filled the small apartment, cool air drifting', but the heat still sat low. Florida heat don't just dip 'cause the sun set.   Same way this block don't just quiet 'cause they had a moment.

Nia leaned back faint, her forehead easing' off Jay's, but her hand stayed pressed light to his chest, fingers curling' in the fabric of   his hoodie. His heartbeat steady under her palm.

Jay's eyes stayed locked on hers — soft,   steady, real. A quiet promise laced behind 'em. No speeches, no fronting'. Just presence. Just him.

The apartment buzzed low — fridge humming', AC kicking', faint clatter of ice shifting' in the freezer. But outside, the block still hummed. The window cracked faint, voices drifting' through. Not loud. But real.

"She still wit' him…"

"Marcus gonna' act up…"

"That girl bold…"

The words curled under   the door,   crawling' through the walls,   quiet, dangerous.

Jay's thumb brushed slow at her waist, anchoring' her, keeping' her rooted in the now. In him. In this.

"You good?" he asked again — voice low,   real, cutting' through the heavy quiet.

Nia's throat worked — pride bruised,   fear still creeping' — but her heart was steady now, her body already leaning' into him.

"We good," she answered — voice low, honest.

Jay's stare softened — not   the playful kinda soft, the real kinda soft. The kind that said I see all your mess and I still want it.

"For real?" he pressed — same tone, steady, no space for fronting'.

Nia's hand slid higher, fingers curling' faint against his hoodie strings, her eyes lifting', her voice coming' quiet but sharp. "For real," she whispered.

The quiet stretched, filled with nerves, want, history. The tension eased, but the weight still floated, still pressed through the walls.   A car engine rumbled past, bass shaking' low. A shout echoed sharp down the block. Laughter curled faint around the corner.

Jay eased back, his hand sliding' down to rest light on her hip — not letting' go, just letting' space breathe.

"We still got a block to face," he muttered, his mouth curving', but his eyes staying' real.

Nia's chest squeezed, her pulse knocking' low, but her pride stayed steady. Her choice? Planted.

"I know," she breathed. "But I ain't facing' it alone."

Jay's thumb grazed her hip, warm, steady. "Nah," he whispered back. "You ain't."

The block was still messy. Still loud. But them? Moving' through it.

Together.

"Marcus Make His Move"

The sidewalk stretched wide under   their steps — pavement   cracked, streetlights buzzing' low, the faint hiss of tires rolling' down uneven asphalt. Nia's arms stayed tight   across her   chest, hoodie sleeves twisted high, nerves crawling' cold up her spine, heart pounding' low behind her ribs. Jay walked steady beside her — broad frame relaxed, chain tucked, shoulders loose — but his eyes? Moving'.   Sharp. Reading' every inch of the street like it been speaking' to him all his life.

The block   was still humming', but different now. Thicker. Watching'. Waiting'.

They passed the corner lot — porch chairs empty, porch lights off, familiar faces peeled back into shadows. And then — Marcus.

Planted outside the liquor store, leaned sharp against the brick wall, hoodie zipped halfway, chain glinting' faint under the weak streetlamp. But it ain't casual. Ain't coincidence. It's placed. Intentional. Like every step he took tonight led him right here. His eyes already locked — not wide, not loud — but sharp, focused, cold enough to raise the hairs on Nia's arms.

Jay clocked it   before Marcus even moved — his hand slid low to Nia's waist, firm, steady. Nia's chest squeezed, nerves twisting', but her feet still moved. Still planted.

Marcus straightened slow, no rush, pushing' off the wall, hands slid into his hoodie pockets.   His mouth curved faint   — not   amused. Calculated. Controlled. The kind of smile folks wear when they already know they in your head.

"Evening'," Marcus tossed, voice low, layered, heavy with quiet challenge.

Jay's jaw flexed, posture steady, eyes locked. "Evening'," he fired back, calm, real, no room for bluffing'.

Nia's breath stuck tight in her chest — pride bruised, nerves crawling' — but her body already slid to Jay's side, already leaning' steady.

Marcus's eyes drifted to her,   lingered, then slid back to Jay,   sharp. "Y'all moving' like y'all built for this," he said, smooth, cutting' through the heavy air. "I see it."

Jay's stare didn't budge, his hand anchored firm at Nia's waist. "We moving' how we move," he answered, voice low, final.

The street held still. Even the usual porch chatter quieted down. The block leaning' in. Waiting'. Clocking'.

Marcus stepped in — not close enough to touch, but close enough to press the energy heavy between 'em.   "You bold," he muttered, eyes sliding' sharp between them. "But this block? It don't love nobody for long."

The words landed — low, heavy, dangerous.

Jay's eyes stayed locked — no flinch, no shake — his presence steady as concrete. "We still here," he said, voice cut low, layered with quiet, real intent. "And we staying'.

"Marcus's grin curved sharper — not joy, not peace — just that quiet threat dressed pretty in a smile. "We gone' see," he muttered, voice low, final, like he already laid the next move down on the board.

He eased back slow, steps drifting' down the lot, his eyes never breaking' off them, that same calculated calm stitched across his face. The message? Loud. The threat? Real. The next play? Already setting' up.

And the block? Still watching'. Still clocking'. Waiting' to see if Nia and Jay gonna' fold — or gonna' stand.

The sidewalk stretched long behind them — cracked pavement,   weak streetlights spilling' dull glow across the lot. But the weight? It still   pressed close. Thick. Heavy. Real.

Jay's hand stayed firm at   Nia's waist — his eyes slid sharp across the block, reading' every corner, every glance that   lingered too long.   Nia's chest stayed tight,   nerves crawling',   pride bruised, but her feet? Still planted. Her body? Still steady beside his.

The hum of the block drifted in — porch chairs creaking', the faint echo of laughter — but under it? That tension. That   shift. The eyes. All of it riding' heavy on the air.

Nia exhaled slow, her hand slid faint to Jay's wrist, her voice low, rough. "He ain't playing'," she muttered.

Jay's jaw flexed faint, his presence steady. "Nah," he answered, quiet, final. "But neither are we."

They passed the liquor   store, two unfamiliar faces still posted near the corner, eyes tracking' them down the lot.   Jay clocked 'em — his stance loose, chest steady, his hand never leaving' Nia's side.

The block rearranged — folks pulling'   into place. Some leaning' quiet for Marcus. Some staying' neutral. A few watching' with quiet respect tucked behind their stares. But the message? Clear.   Ain't no room for   slipping' now.

Nia's pride flared faint,   her hand curling' light at Jay's hoodie sleeve,   her voice low. "I'm tired of   this feeling',"   she admitted — real,   raw, nerves twisting' under her words.

Jay's eyes slid to hers — steady,   honest. "Me too," he answered. "But we stay ready."

The words settled heavy, warm, honest. Not loud. But enough.

The lot stretched ahead — porch lights flickering',   the block buzzing', the pressure heavy. But them? Still moving'. Still together. Still ready.

CHAPTER 17

"Block Can't Break What's Solid"

The heat still hung thick on the lot   — pavement hot under their shoes, streetlights buzzing', the sky stretching' deep blue over the rooftops.   The block buzzed louder now.   Porches full. Folks leaned on fences.   Kids ran down the sidewalk, sneakers smacking' concrete. But under the hum? Tension. Twisting'. Real.

Nia walked close to Jay — hoodie sleeves slid high,   arms folded tight across her chest, nerves crawling' raw under her skin. Jay moved steady — broad frame loose,   shoulders relaxed, but his eyes? Sharp. Clocking'. Reading' every face, every glance that lingered too long. They cut down the corner lot   — the   liquor store ahead, porch chairs creaking', conversations hushing' as they passed.

And then — Marcus.

Planted on the corner, posted up bold, leaning' casual on a car door, arms crossed, hoodie zipped halfway,   his crew flanked behind him.   This ain't subtle. This ain't quiet. This? Planned.   Loud. Public. His eyes already locked on them — sharp, steady, pride layered heavy behind his stare.

Jay's jaw flexed faint,   his hand slid to Nia's waist,   firm, anchoring' her. Nia's pulse jumped — pride bruising',   nerves twisting' — but her feet stayed planted, her body already leaning' close to Jay. Marcus straightened slow, his mouth curved sharp,   the block leaning' in like this the show they been waiting' on.

"Look at y'all," Marcus fired, voice loud, riding' across the street. "Moving' like y'all own this." Jay's stare never wavered — shoulders loose,   stance steady. "We moving' how we move," he shot   back, voice low but cutting' through the air.

The crowd shifted — folks slid to porches,   eyes glued, mouths pressed tight. Nia's heart twisted, her gaze flicking' across the street   — every neighbor, every cousin clocking' the scene. Marcus stepped off the car, slow, smooth. His eyes slid to her now, lingered heavy.

"You proud of   this?" he tossed, words sharp, layered with history and bruised pride. "This what you riding' with?"

Nia's breath stuck in her chest — pride, fear, love knotted tight behind her ribs. Jay's hand stayed steady, his voice coming' low, real.

"She made her choice," Jay muttered, final. Real.

The words cracked the moment — block leaning' closer, whispers riding' the air. Marcus's jaw flexed, his smile curling' sharp, dangerous. "Then y'all better stay ready," he muttered — voice low, a promise dressed in threat.

The quiet stretched, tension sharp, then Marcus eased back. His crew slid with him, eyes still heavy on them as he drifted down the lot. But the block? Still buzzing'. Still watching'. Still loud. And the test? Just hit full force.

The street buzzed hot with noise — old porch chairs creaking', car doors slamming', faint music riding' low on the breeze.   But under all that? Tension. Twisting'. Loud. Heavy. Visible now.

Nia walked close to Jay — arms crossed,   hoodie sleeves bunched at her elbows, pride crawling' raw under her skin. Her eyes drifted down the lot — porch to porch, stoop to stoop — every stare that   lingered, every glance that cut sharp through the air. Jay's hand stayed light at   her waist, fingers pressing' faint but steady. His shoulders loose, but his presence? Heavy. Real. Unshaken.

Ms. Carter sat perched on her   stoop, hand-fan slowing', mouth pressed tight, eyes following' them long, layered with judgment   but maybe a little quiet respect tucked behind it. Further down, Kia leaned on the porch rail — arms folded, eyes sharp, head tilted faint as they crossed her   line of sight.

"They bold," Kia muttered low, half to herself, half for them. "Bout time."

Nia's chest squeezed — pride bruised, nerves twisting'   — but her feet still planted.

Keisha posted near the corner, phone in hand,   mouth curved faint, eyes sliding' to Nia, then to Jay. "Hope you solid," Keisha tossed,   voice riding' low under her breath. "You gone' need to be."

Jay's jaw flexed faint, his eyes sweeping' the block, hand curling' tighter at Nia's side. They passed Mr. Ellis's store — the usual card game paused on the sidewalk, old heads leaning' back, arms crossed, eyes watching'. One nodded faint, respect quiet but there. The other? Mouth tight, gaze slid cold across Jay's frame, then to Nia.

Nia's pulse twisted — her pride and fear knocking'   against each other — but her hand already slid to Jay's wrist,   anchoring' herself there. Jay's voice cracked low, just for her.

"Block showing' their hand now," he muttered, steady, real.

Nia exhaled slow, her eyes cut sharp around the lot.   "They always been showing' it," she answered, voice rough. "We just seeing' it clear."

The sidewalk stretched long — porch lights flickering',   folks leaning' in, conversations low but   eyes loud. Some nodding' faint, respect tucked behind the quiet.   Some mouths curled tight,   eyes slid sharp with quiet judgment. Some leaning' on Marcus's side — subtle colors, familiar faces acting' funny, bodies posting' up in spots they ain't   never cared about till now.

Lines drawn. Sides picked. No more maybe. No more whispers. Just... clear.

Jay's thumb grazed her   waist — small,   steady. "Easier that way," he muttered.

Nia's pride bruised, but her body leaned into his,   steady, solid. The block rearranged. The noise settled sharp.   The lines bold now. But them? Still moving'. Still together.

The door clicked shut soft behind them — metal   latch falling' in place — but the air inside? Thick. Heavy. Louder than it should be. The hum of the AC buzzed low, but it barely touched the heat   pressed into the walls — block heat, pride heat, family heat.

Nia eased in slow — hoodie sleeves pushed high,   arms crossed, nerves crawling' low up her spine. Her pulse twisted sharp behind her ribs,   pride bruising' raw, fear simmering' just under her skin. Jay's frame moved steady behind her — broad shoulders loose, chain tucked under his hoodie — but his eyes? Moving'. Clocking' the room same way he clocked the block.

Brenda stood at the kitchen counter — dish towel twisted in her hand, arms folded, eyes heavy, mouth tight. Kia perched on the arm of   the couch — legs crossed, one brow raised,   stare slid sharp between them.   Keisha leaned by the fridge — phone in hand, thumb frozen mid-scroll, her stare locking' hard on Jay like he the only thing in the room worth clocking'.

The hum of the fridge clicked faint, old floorboards creaked low — but the silence pressed thick. Brenda's voice cracked it first — sharp, layered, ain't no question in it.

"He loud out there," Brenda fired — eyes on Nia, her words riding' tight with that old head mama-tone. "And y'all just strolling' through like this block won't swallow you whole."

Nia's chest squeezed — pride curled sharp, nerves twisting' — but her feet still moving', already squared up, already leaning' into Jay's steady warmth at her side.

Kia exhaled a sharp chuckle — cousin-tone layered in every word.   "She ain't hiding' no more," Kia tossed — voice low, blunt. "Ain't no turning' back after that show outside."

Keisha's eyes cut to Jay — sharp, quiet, testing'. "You good with all this attention?" she asked, voice low but slid with challenge. "This ain't just block whispers now — they watching' y'all like it's cable."

Jay's jaw flexed faint, his stance unshaken, hand slid to Nia's waist, thumb pressing' light, steady. "We ain't here for the block," he answered — voice low, real, layered with the weight of somebody that seen enough mess to know better. "We here for each other."

The words hung in the room — thick,   sharp, unarguable — but Brenda's stare stayed locked, heavy, carrying' every ounce of love, fear, and history wrapped tight around her pride.

"You gonna' need more than each other," Brenda warned — voice softer now, but real, honest. "This ain't some storybook. This block? It eat folks that ain't ready."

The AC hummed faint.   The window buzzed with faint   block noise. But in here? It was just them. Just the heat. Just the words.

Nia's throat worked — pride bruised,   nerves crawling' — but her voice cracked rough, steady. "I know," Nia answered — eyes cut   to Jay, then back to her mama. "But that's where we start."

The silence stretched — floor creaking', old fridge clicking', the hum of the outside floating' faint — but inside, the air pressed tight.

Kia's eyes softened — barely — her arms uncrossing', mouth curving' faint with quiet respect tucked behind her cousin-shade. Keisha stayed leaning' by the fridge — eyes sharp,   still testing', but the words stayed down for now. Brenda sighed slow,   arms uncrossing', her stare shifting' softer, layered with that tired mama-love that ain't ever really quiet.

"This ain't easy," Brenda muttered — voice rough,   real, pride tangled in every word. "But you picked your side. Stand in it."

Nia's pride flared, her feet firm, her body leaning'   in closer to Jay's steady frame. "We standing'," she answered, voice sharp, low, unshaken. Jay's hand stayed steady at her side, warmth pressing' in, his presence louder than all the mouths in the room.

The block? Loud.   The house? Messy.   But them? Still   standing'. Still moving'. Together.

The hum of the AC drifted low — the quiet tick of the fridge, the faint rattle of the window — but the house was settling', finally. Brenda disappeared down the hall, her sigh still hanging' heavy in the air, footsteps soft as she moved back to her room. Kia stretched out on the couch — phone slid to the side, her eyes drifting' half-shut, mouth finally quiet. Keisha stayed leaning' by the counter — still clocking', still watching' — but her words tucked away now, her stare sliding' off them slow as she turned back to her screen.

Nia eased toward the window — arms folded, hoodie sleeves bunched at her wrists, her breath slow, chest tight. Jay followed — steps quiet, presence steady, hand sliding' soft to her waist.

Outside? The block still buzzing'. Porch chairs creaking'. Voices drifting'. Bass humming' low from a car parked crooked by the lot. But in here? For the first time all day? It was just them. Just breath. Just quiet.

Nia leaned faint into Jay's side — her pride still bruised, her nerves still crawling' low — but her body already resting' on his. Already staying'. Jay's hand stayed firm at her waist, thumb slid slow along her side, his breath steady beside hers.

"We still good?" he asked, voice low, rough, for her alone.

Nia's throat worked — her eyes slid to him, her hand drifting' up to his hoodie sleeve. "We still good," she answered — voice rough, tired, real.

The words settled soft between 'em — not loud, not rushed — but steady. Jay's mouth curved faint — not a smile, something' softer, heavier.

"This ain't easy," he muttered, voice real, low.

Nia's breath dragged slow,   her head leaning' faint against his shoulder. "Wasn't expecting' easy," she whispered. "Just real."

The outside noise carried on — the block humming', the streets shifting'   — but in here? Just steady breath. Just quiet hands. Just… solid.

The love? Tested.   But staying'. The block? Loud.   But it couldn't break what's solid

CHAPTER 18

"We Built This"

The hum of the fan buzzed low from the window — Florida heat already creeping in, sunlight stretching soft across the worn floorboards. The apartment sat quiet. Not heavy quiet. Just… steady.

Nia eased into the small kitchen — hoodie slid off, tank top clinging to her ribs, pride settled low in her chest. The coffee pot clicked faint as it brewed, warm smell drifting through the room. Outside, the block was already awake — porch doors creaking, old heads posted by the fence, voices carrying, music floating soft from a cracked window. But under it all, the tension felt different now. Eased. Not gone — but shifted.

Her bare feet padded across the cool linoleum, fingers pulling down mismatched mugs. She caught her reflection faint in the window — sleep still tucked under her eyes, but her shoulders were squared, chest steady. A regular morning, but it wasn't so regular anymore.

Her phone buzzed faint on the counter — a text from Kia: Block still watching'. But they quieter now.

Nia's mouth curved faint, pride tangled with quiet nerves. She poured coffee slow, steam rising, her eyes sliding to the window. Across the lot, Jay was posted up — broad shoulders relaxed, hoodie zipped halfway, chain tucked. But his eyes? Sharp. Moving. Clocking every shadow, every glance.

Her chest squeezed, not with fear, but with fullness — pride, steady love, knowing they were still standing. The coffee cup was warm in her hand, sunlight spilling across her, the block humming outside. For the first time, it didn't sink her. It was just there. And so was she.

The pavement stretched wide — cracked lines running through the lot, patches of grass pushing up between breaks in the concrete. The block buzzed low with porch voices and faint music drifting from down the street, but the air still held weight. Watchful.

Jay leaned against the corner fence, one hand in his pocket, hoodie sleeves shoved to his elbows. His stance looked easy, but his eyes stayed moving, clocking everything. Marcus's crew lingered near the liquor store — three of them, posted casual, but mouths quiet now. Their glances slid his way, but they weren't loud like before. They moved cautious, watching the way he held the block without even saying a word.

Across the lot, porch curtains shifted — Ms.   Carter peeked out, her fan pausing midair, mouth pressed tight. The old heads by the fence nodded slow as Jay passed, respect buried in weathered stares. Nia caught it all from the window — coffee warming her palms, eyes fixed on him. Her chest tightened, pride twisting, nerves buzzing faint but steady under it.

A car rolled slow down the block,   bass humming, tinted windows cracked just enough to catch eyes.   Jay's posture never shifted. His gaze tracked the plates, the faces. Calm. Concrete. Unshaken. The car eased past, the block kept humming, and Jay stayed rooted — like nothing could move him.

When his eyes finally slid up to hers, catching her in the window, his mouth curved faint. Not a smile. Something heavier. Real. Her heart thudded slow, feet already itching toward the door. The block could whisper, could watch, but Jay wasn't folding. And for the first time, Nia knew — neither was she.

The apartment door clicked soft behind them later that   night, the outside noise still humming low — porch chairs creaking, faint music drifting — but in here it was just them. Just quiet. Just breath.

Nia slid to the counter,   mug warm in her palms,   her eyes wandering the chipped cabinets and crooked blinds. Pride curled low in her chest anyway. Jay leaned on the doorway,   hoodie half off, chain glinting faint.   For a moment, neither spoke. The air stretched easy between them. Comfortable.

"We gotta fix that back window," Nia said finally, her voice rough but steady, eyes cutting to the crooked frame spilling sunlight sideways.

Jay chuckled low, broad shoulders relaxing. "Window ain't gonna'   hold this block out," he tossed back.

Nia's mouth curved faint. "Ain't trying' to hold it out. Just keep the rain off my floor."

His laugh broke soft, warm. Then his gaze shifted, words dropping quieter. "We could… look at something' else. Get out this side of the block. Just… start clean."

Her chest tightened — nerves crawling,   pride twisting, but hope flickered small and real under it. "Start clean, or run?" she asked.

"Start clean, together," Jay answered, steady, unshaken. "Ain't running'. Just building' something' ours. Somewhere they can't reach."

The air stilled — fridge humming, window buzzing faint. The future crept in.

Nia exhaled slow, her hand sliding to his wrist.   "Messy apartments. Bad blinds. Leaky windows."

Jay's mouth curved, eyes soft. "Long as it's ours."

Her chest loosened, her feet steady. The block could stay buzzing outside. In here, they were already building.

Later, the porch stretched wide beneath their   feet — old wood creaking, paint chipped from years of weather. The Florida night eased warm, a faint breeze sliding over the lot. The block hummed background noise — porch music soft, laughter spilling, curtains shifting.

Nia leaned against the rail, arms folded, hoodie sleeves bunched. She took in the familiar cracks in the sidewalk,   busted porch lights down the way, crooked cars parked along the curb.   It all looked different   tonight. Or maybe she did.

Jay stood beside her   — hands tucked, chain glinting faint. His presence steady, louder than the hum of the street. His eyes swept the block like always, clocking every movement.   Marcus's people were gone,   the old heads were quiet, and the block itself buzzed softer now. Respect hanging in the air, unspoken but real.

Nia breathed deep — the block's smell   of cut grass and old pavement pressing in. "We still here," she muttered.

Jay's mouth curved faint, eyes sharp. "We still standing'."

The porch held quiet, floorboards groaning under their shift. She leaned into his side, his hand sliding to her wrist, thumb resting light on her pulse. The hum of the block kept moving outside, but here it was just them.

Nia's eyes found his, raw and honest. "This block ain't gonna' make it easy."

His thumb brushed her wrist. "We ain't built for easy," he said, quiet but final. "We built for standing'."

The words dropped heavy, unshakable. Her chest loosened. Feet planted. Body already leaning into him.

The porch lights flickered faint, block still buzzing, but the space they stood in was theirs. Messy. Unfinished. But solid.

Jay's voice came low. "We gonna' build more. Ain't stopping' here."

Her breath left slow, his words wrapping around her like armor.

The block still watched. Still breathed. But tonight, this porch, this love, this steady? It was theirs. Not perfect. Not easy. But real.

They built this. Together.